Joaquin Miller

My Own Story

Joaquin Miller

My Own Story

ISBN/EAN: 9783744747141

Printed in Europe, USA, Canada, Australia, Japan

Cover: Foto ©Andreas Hilbeck / pixelio.de

More available books at **www.hansebooks.com**

Yours.
Joaquin Miller.

MY
OWN
STORY

BY

JOAQUIN MILLER,

AUTHOR OF

"SONGS OF THE SIERRAS," "THE DANITES,"
"THE ONE FAIR WOMAN,"
"49," ETC., ETC.

CHICAGO:
BELFORD-CLARKE CO., PUBLISHERS.
1890.

I Dedicate this Book

to

The Dearest Friend of My Life in the Sierras

and

Later Wanderings in the Old World,

Colonel JAMES VAUGHN THOMAS,

of Leon, Nicaragua,

Who is Named and Known in these Pages as

"THE PRINCE."

PREFACE.

THIS book is the story of my life among the Indians; and yet it is not the story, not the half of it — hardly the hundredth part of it — for each day of those four years was of itself a volume. Personal peril and adventure I have left out largely, because bigger and better things are before us in the sublime scenery and the poetry and pathos of a voiceless race.

It is a marvel that the writer, with his impetuosity (want of common sense), survived even a portion of those days. For example, returning weary and half-blinded by the snow from an unsuccessful hunt, a chasm was encountered. His companions picked their way cautiously around; but he audaciously tried to leap it. By the sheerest chance he struck a narrow ledge some twenty feet below, and was fished out by his Indian companions. But his hat and gun are still in that bottomless chasm of Mount Shasta.

Similar incidents by flood and flame, to say nothing of wild beasts and wilder men, both white and red, dot nearly every one of those eventful and most glorious days. But let us lift our faces above them.

I was living in London at the outbreak of the Modoc war, and it having become known, through the " Songs of the Sierras," that I had once lived with those people, and neighboring tribes, the writers from the seat of war gave most wild and romantic accounts of my early history.

It was said that I was the real Joaquin Murrietta, who had escaped with a price on his head to the mountains. No one seemed to understand why a man should seek to live in the heart of the Sierras for any other purpose than that of plunder. Meantime the demand for books or stories about these Indians, the Modoc war, and the cause of it, was very great in London.

To throw the fictions of these imaginative writers, and the facts as set forth in a few sketches already written, into a book, was the work of a few weeks. A war of extermination, it seemed to me, was being waged against my best friends, and it was imperative that I should strike hard and at once. And so, in great haste, and with a confusion of fact and fiction, a volume was brought out by the Queen's Publisher. The first edition was dedicated to Wendell Phillips, and that great orator and humanitarian mounted the forum for the Red Man, as he had for the Black Man.

The author expected this book to quietly die when it had done its work; but, as it seems determined to outlive him, with all its follies and fictions, he has taken it severely in hand, cut off all its fictitious growth, and confined its leaves to the cold, frozen truth: " the truth, and nothing but the truth," if not " the whole truth."

JOAQUIN MILLER.

THE HEIGHTS, OAKLAND, CAL., 1890.

CONTENTS.

MY OWN STORY.

CHAPTER I.

A PREFATORY UNDERSTANDING.

THERE are Indians and Indians. A man may fight for some Indians, and fight against other Indians, and yet not be at all in the wrong. At Waterloo, France and England were not friendly. But in the Crimean war, less than half a century later, they stood shoulder to shoulder. If conditions of this sort can exist among the most civilized nations, it ought not to be counted so very inconsistent if a boy, thrown among savages, should, in the course of his duty, or even desire, or perhaps in the course of what might really be called "diplomacy," be found fighting at one time for and with a certain tribe of Indians, and at another time against another tribe of Indians. And yet an ungrateful and forgetful world will perhaps continue to insist that for years the writer of this sketch was a savage among savages, and only there for blood and plunder. How cruelly wrong!

Let it be said, in a single paragraph, that the hand which pens these lines has been raised in six several campaigns for the white men against Indians; that the writer was three times terribly wounded in these wars.

Some of these battles were fought in Oregon, some in Idaho, some in California. Some are matters of record; but for the most part they are perishing from the memory of man, as the pioneers who bore part with him are perishing from the earth. However, there is one brief record which bears the great seal of the State of California. It is given here because it is brief; not at all because it shows the writer to the best advantage, for this it surely does not; because in the other expeditions he was the leader, and led in name as well as in spirit, while here he is set down as a private soldier.

HEADQUARTERS ADJUTANT GENERAL'S OFFICE,
STATE OF CALIFORNIA,
SACRAMENTO, CAL., December 15, 1883.

Joaquin Miller, New York.

DEAR SIR—In answer to your letter addressed to General, now Governor, Stoneman, I have to say that I find on examination of the records on file in this office that you served as a volunteer in one of the early Modoc wars, known as the "Pitt River Expedition," from March the 16th, 1857, to May the 2d, 1857, for forty-eight days. It also appears that you furnished your own horse and equipments. It further appears that you are the only one who took part in said expedition that never received any compensation for his services. The fault is probably your own, in not applying for it. But now, after the lapse of more than a quarter of a century, there is no money in the Treasury for the payment of such claims. Your remedy is by special act of the Legislature of the State of California.

Respectfully yours,

GEO. B. CROSBY,
Adjutant General for the State of California.

[Seal of California.]

As if I had asked for a certificate of this record for the money there was in it! Still, let some young financier who is apt at arithmetic stop here and calculate how much this one State, to say nothing of Idaho, Oregon, Arizona and the Federal States also, might be owing me now in gold coin. For I never, from any one, or from any source whatever, accepted one cent for my services. Take this one account of California, which she frankly says, under the great seal, is due me, and see what it would amount to at an annual interest for more than thirty years. The pay allowed was five dollars per day for horse and equipments; the same for a man. But compute and compound, after ascertaining the amount due at the rate of ten dollars per day, for " forty-eight days." You will find that a certain great State is owing to a certain humble person nearly all the gold on the great glittering dome of her capitol. Let her people, then—her strong,

new people, who are pushing us older ones off the
globe—not be too eager to accuse and find fault
with the work I have done until that work is in
some sort paid for. But now, in order to tell my
own true story of my life among the Indians, about
which so very much has been written, and about
which so very little is known, I must turn back to
the beginning.

A most romantic and restless boy, I ran away
from school in Oregon at the age of thirteen to the
gold mines of California.

The scene of this narrative lies immediately about
the base of Mount Shasta. The   Klamat River
with its tributaries flows from its snows on the
north, and the quiet Sacramento from the south.
The Shasta Indians, now but the remnant of a tribe
at one time the most powerful on the Pacific, live
at the south base of the mountain, while the Modoc and Pitt River Indians live at the east and
northeast, with the Klamats still to the north.

It was late in the fall. I do not know the day
or even remember the month; but I do know that
I was alone, a frail, sensitive, girl-looking boy,
almost destitute, trying to make my way to the
mines of California, and that before I had ridden
my little spotted cayuse pony half way up the ten-

FIRST VIEW OF SHASTA.

mile trail that then crossed the Siskiyou Mountains, I met little patches of snow; and that a keen,
cold wind came pitching down between the trees
into my face from the California side of the summit.

At one place I saw where a moccasin track was
in the snow, and leading across the trail; a very
large track I thought it was then, but now I know
that it was made by many feet stepping in the same
impression.

My dress was scant enough for winter, and it
was chill and dismal. A fantastic dress, too, for
one looking to the rugged life of a miner; a sort
of cross between an Indian chief and a Mexican
vaquero, with a preference for color carried to ex-
tremes.

As I approached the summit the snow grew
deeper, and the dark firs, weighted with snow,
reached their sable and supple limbs across my
path as if to catch me by the yellow hair, that fell,
like a school-girl's, on my shoulders. Some of the
little firs were covered with snow, and were con-
verted into pyramids and snowy pillars.

I lifted my eyes, and looked away to the south.
Mount Shasta was before me. For the first time
I now looked upon the mountain in whose shadows

so many tragedies were to be enacted; the most comely and perfect snow peak in America. Nearly a hundred miles away, it seemed, in the pure, clear atmosphere of the mountains, to be almost at hand. Above the woods, above the clouds, almost above the earth, it looked like the first approach of land to another world. Away across a gray sea of clouds that arose from the Klamat and Shasta Rivers, the mountain stood, a solitary island ; white and flashing like a pyramid of silver ! solemn and majestic, sublime! lonely and cold and white. A cloud or two about his brow, sometimes resting there, then wreathed and coiled about, then blown like banners streaming in the wind.

I had lifted my hands to Mount Hood, uncovered my head, bowed down and felt unutterable things, loved, admired, adored, with all the strength of an impulsive and passionate young heart. But he who loves and worships naturally and freely, as all strong, true souls must and will do, loves that which is most magnificent and most lovable in his scope of vision. Hood is a magnificent idol ; is sufficient, if you do not see Shasta.

A grander or a lovelier object makes shipwreck of a former love. This is sadly so.

Jealousy is born of an instinctive knowledge of this truth.

Hood is rugged, kingly, majestic, terrible! But he is only the head and front of a well-raised family. He is not alone in his splendor. Your admiration is divided and weakened. Beyond the Columbia St. Helen's flashes in the sun in summer, or is folded in clouds from the sea in winter. On either hand Jefferson and Washington divide the attention; then farther away, fair as a stud of fallen stars, the white Three Sisters are grouped together about the fountain springs of the Willamette River;—all in a line—all in one range of mountains; as it were, mighty milestones along the way of clouds!—marble pillars pointing the road to God.

Mount Shasta has all the sublimity, all the strength, majesty and magnificence of Hood; yet is so alone, unsupported and solitary, that you go down before him utterly, with an undivided adoration—a sympathy for his loneliness and a devotion for his valor—an admiration that shall pass unchallenged.

CHAPTER II.

AS LONE as God, and white as a winter moon, Mount Shasta starts up sudden and solitary from the heart of the great black forests of Northern California.

You would hardly call Mount Shasta a part of the Sierras; you would say rather that it is the great white tower of some ancient and eternal wall, with nearly all the white walls overthrown.

It has no rival! There is not even a snow-crowned subject in sight of its dominion. A shining pyramid in mail of everlasting frosts and ice, the sailor sometimes, in a day of singular clearness, catches glimpses of it from the sea a hundred miles away to the west; and it may be seen from the dome of the capital 340 miles distant. The immigrant coming from the east beholds the snowy, solitary pillar from afar out on the arid sage-brush plains, and lifts his hands in silence as in answer to a sign.

Column upon column of storm-stained tamarack, strong-tossing pines, and warlike looking firs have

(18)

rallied here. They stand with their backs against this mountain, frowning down dark-browed, and confronting the face of the Saxon. They defy the advance of civilization into their ranks. What if these dark and splendid columns, a hundred miles in depth, should be the last to go down in America! What if this should be the old guard gathered here, marshaled around their emperor in plumes and armor, that may die but not surrender!

Ascend this mountain, stand against the snow above the upper belt of pines, and take a glance below. Toward the sea nothing but the black and unbroken forest. Mountains, it is true, dip and divide and break the monotony as the waves break up the sea; yet it is still the sea, still the unbroken forest, black and magnificent. To the south the landscape sinks and declines gradually, but still maintains its column of dark-plumed grenadiers, till the Sacramento Valley is reached, nearly a hundred miles away. Silver rivers run here, the sweetest in the world. They wind and wind among the rocks and mossy roots, with California lilies, and the yew with scarlet berries dipping in the water, and trout idling in the eddies and cool places by the basketful. On the east, the forest still keeps up unbroken

women without mercy, men without reason, brand them with the appropriate name of savages.

I have a word to say for the Indian. I saw him as he was, not as he is. In one little spot of our land, I saw him as he was centuries ago in every part of it perhaps, a Druid and a dreamer —the mildest and the tamest of beings. I saw him as no man can see him now. I saw him as no man ever saw him who had the desire and patience to observe, the sympathy to understand, and the intelligence to communicate his observations to those who would really like to understand him. He is truly " the gentle savage ; " the worst and the best of men, the tamest and the fiercest of beings. The world cannot understand the combination of these two qualities. For want of truer comparison let us liken him to a woman —a sort of Parisian woman, now made desperate by a long siege and an endless war.

A singular combination of circumstances laid his life bare to me. I was a child, and he was a child. He permitted me to enter his heart.

CHAPTER III.

MY FIRST BATTLE.

As I DESCENDED the stupendous and steep mountain that fronted the matchless and magnificent glory of Mount Shasta, I fell in with an old mountaineer by the name of " Mountain Joe," one of Fremont's former guides, who was on his way with a small party of Mexicans to the Rio Grande to get a band of wild, or rather half-wild, Mexican horses.

I was a timid lad, friendless and almost penniless. I got acquainted with the old mountaineer, as our roads lay together, and was glad to accept his offer to go along and become a vaquero.

Soon we reached his ranch, Soda Springs, on the headwaters of the Sacramento river, and here sat down to rest and recruit our horses.

We had not been here long, however, till a band of hostile Indians descended from Castle Rocks, during our temporary absence, and not only plundered our camp, but burned it to the ground.

The few gold hunters along the river formed a company, and, along with some friendly Indians, all

under the lead of Mountain Joe, stealthily followed the hostile savages up into their very strong
and seemingly impregnable fortress; and there I
saw my first real battle with Indians.

This " castle " is the most picturesque object in all
the magnificent scenery of northern California.   It
sits on a high mountain, and is formed of gray
granite blocks and spires, lifting singly and in
groups thousands of feet from the summit of the
mountain.   Most of these are inaccessible.   Here
the Indians locate the abode of the devil.   Hence
its name, " the Devil's Castle."

All of us were on foot, as the Castle cannot be
approached by horsemen.   We reached Castle
Lake, a sweet, peaceful place, overhung by mountain cypress and sweeping cedars, without adventure.
This is a spot the Indians will not visit, for fear of
the evil spirits which they are certain inhabit the
place.   Our Indian allies sat down in the wood
overlooking the lake, while we descended, drank
of the cool, deep water, and refreshed ourselves
for the combat, since the spies had just returned
and reported the hostile camp only an hour distant.   The enemy was not dreaming of our approach, and we were in position, almost surround-
ing the camp, before we were discovered.

When we came near, Mountain Joe distributed us behind the rocks and trees in range of and overlooking the camp. The ground was all densely timbered, and covered with a thick growth of black, stiff chaparral, save one spot of a few acres, by the side of which the Indians were camped, at the foot of a little hill.

I was placed by Mountain Joe behind a large pine, and alone. He spoke kindly as he left me, and bade me take care of myself.

I put some bullets in my mouth, and made all preparation to do my part. It seemed like an age before the fight began. I could hear my heart beat like a little drum.

The Indians certainly had not the least suspicion of danger. They were, it seemed, as much off their guard as possible. They evidently thought their camp, if not impregnable, beyond our reach and discovery. They owed the latter to their own race.

At last we were discerned, as some of the most daring and experienced were stealing closer and closer to the camp, and the wild Indians sprang to their arms with whoops and yells that lifted my hat almost from my head.

The yells were answered.   Rifles cracked around the camp, and arrows came back in showers.

" Close up ! " shouted Mountain Joe, and we left cover and advanced.   I think I must have swallowed the bullets I had put in my mouth, for I loaded from my pouch as usual, and thought of the bullets in my mouth no more as we moved down upon the yelling Indians.

A little group of us gathered behind some rocks. Then a man came creeping to us through the brush to say that the other side of our company was being pressed.   Then another came to say that Mountain Joe had been struck across the face by an arrow, and his eyes were so injured that he could not direct the fight.

We wound our blankets about our breasts and bodies, so as to guard against arrows, but our heads were unprotected.

Suddenly the arrows came, whiz, whistle, thud, right in our faces.

I fell senseless.   After a while I felt men pulling me by my shoulders.   I could hear and understand but could not see or rise.   It seemed to me they were trying to twist my neck from my body.   Yet I felt no great pain, only a numbness and utter helplessness.

" Help me pull it out," said one. They pulled.

" No, you must cut off the point, and then pull it back."

Then they cut and pulled, and the blood spurted out and rattled on the leaves.

" Poor boy, he's done for."

I could now see, but was still helpless. Half a dozen men stood around leaning on their rifles, looking at me, then around them, as if for the enemy, but the little battle was over. By the side of me, with his head in a man's lap, lay a young man, James Lane, with an arrow-shot near the eye. He died of his wound.

An arrow had struck me in the left side of the face, struck the teeth, and then glanced around and came out at the back of the neck. The wound certainly looked as if it must be mortal, but the jugular vein was not touched, and there was hope. I was dizzy, and sometimes senseless. This, perhaps, was because the wound was so near the brain. I constantly thought I was on the mountain slope overlooking home, and kept telling the men to go and bring my mother. We had no surgeon, and the men tied up our wounds as best they could in tobacco saturated in saliva.

That night the Indian camp was plundered and burnt.

In the morning one kind but mistaken old fellow brought a leather bag, and held it up haughtily before my eyes in his left hand, while he tapped it gently with his bowie-knife. The blood was oozing through the seams of the bag, and trickling at his feet.

" Them's scalps."

I grew sick at the sight.

The wounded were carried on the backs of squaws that had been taken in the fight. A very old and wrinkled woman carried me on her back by setting me in a large buckskin, with one leg on each side of her body, and then supporting the weight by a broad leather strap passed across her brow. This was not uncomfortable, all things considered. In fact, it was by far the best thing that could be done.

The first half-day the old woman was " sulky," as the men called it ; possibly the wrinkled old creature could feel, and was thinking of her dead.

In the afternoon I began to rally, and spoke to her in her own tongue. Then she talked and talked, and mourned, and would not be still.

" You," she moaned, " have killed all my boys, and burnt up my home."

I ventured to protest that they had first robbed us.

" No ;" she said, " you first robbed us. You drove us from the river. We could not fish, we could not hunt. We were hungry and took your provisions to eat. My boys did not kill you. They could have killed you a hundred times, but they only took things to eat, when they could not get fish and things on the river."

We reached the Sacramento, and pitched camp on the bank of the river under some sweeping cedars below the site of the present hotel on the Lower Soda Spring ranch. Here I lay till able to travel.

CHAPTER IV.

" EL VAQUERO."

ONCE again in the saddle, we made good time on our well-rested horses, and in a few weeks were on the waters of the Gila River.

We spent the winter in Arizona and Mexico, and by the springtime Mountain Joe and his Mexican friends had a band of horses numbering many hundreds. We made our way back to northern California slowly; for we had much trouble with bad men, who wanted to get money out of the Mexicans. Indeed, they were constantly robbing the Mexicans, either by· process of law, or otherwise. It was almost a daily occurrence for some Americans to swear out a warrant, or other process, accuse the Mexicans of stealing horses, and make them pay heavily, either in money or horses, to be allowed to go on.

Finally, after many losses and much bad luck, Mountain Joe took a few of the remaining horses and returned to his ranch at Soda Springs, near where the battle had been fought, and left me with two. not over good-natured Mexicans.

We reached northern California after a long and lonely journey, through wild and fertile valleys, with only the smoke of wigwams curling from the fringe of trees that hemmed them in, or from the river bank that cleft the little Edens to disprove the fancy that here might have been the Paradise, and here the scene of the expulsion.

· We crossed flashing rivers, still white and clear, that since have become turbid yellow pools with barren banks of boulders, shorn of their overhanging foliage, and drained of flood by ditches that the resolute miner has led even around the mountain tops.

On entering Pitt River Valley we met with thousands of Indians, gathered there for the purpose of fishing, but they kindly assisted us across the two branches of the river, and gave no sign of ill-will.

We pushed far up the valley in the direction of Yreka, and there pitched camp, for the Mexicans wished to recruit their horses on the rich meadows of wild grass before driving them to town for market.

We camped against a high spur of a long, timbered hill, that terminated abruptly at the edge of the valley. A clear stream of water full of trout, with willow-lined banks, wound through the length

of the narrow valley, entirely hidden in the long
grass and leaning willows.

The Pitt River Indians did not visit us here,
neither did the Modocs, and we began to hope we
were entirely hidden, in the deep, narrow little
valley, from all Indians, both friendly and unfriendly,
until one evening some young men, calling themselves Shastas, came into the camp. They were
very friendly, however; were splendid horsemen,
and assisted to bring in and corral the horses like
old vaqueros.

Our force was very small, and the Mexicans
employed two of these young fellows to attend and
keep watch about the horses.

Some weeks wore on pleasantly enough, when
we began to prepare to strike camp for Yreka.
Thus far we had not seen the sign of a Modoc
Indian.

It was early in the morning. The rising sun was
streaming up the valley, through the fringe of fir
and cedar trees. The Indian boys and I had just
returned from driving the herd of horses a little
way down the stream. The two Mexicans were sitting at breakfast, with their backs to the high, bare
wall with its crown of trees. The Indians were
taking our saddle-horses across the little stream to

tether them there on fresh grass, and I was walking
idly toward the camp, only waiting for my tawny
young companions.   Crack ! crash ! thud !

The two men fell on their faces, and never uttered
a word.   Indians were running down the little lava
mountain side, with bows and rifles in their hands,
and the hanging, rugged brow of the hill was curling in smoke.

I started to run, and ran with all my might
toward where I had left the Indian boys. I
remember distinctly thinking how cowardly it
was to run and desert the wounded men, with
the Indians upon them, and I also remember thinking, that, when I got to the first bank of willows,
I would turn and fire, for I had laid hold of
the pistol in my belt, and could have fired, and
should have done so, but I was thoroughly
frightened, and no doubt, if I had succeeded
in reaching the willows, I would have thought it
best to go still further before turning about.

How rapidly one thinks at such a time, and
how distinctly one remembers every thought.

All this, however, was but a flash, the least part
of an instant.   Some mounted Indians that had
been stationed up the valley darted out at the first
shot, and one of them was upon me before I saw

3

him, for I was only concerned with the Indians
pouring down the little hill out of the smoke into
the camp.

I was struck down by a club, or some hard, heavy
object, maybe the pole of a hatchet, possibly only
a horse's hoof.

When I recovered, which must have been some
minutes after, an Indian was rolling me over and
pulling at the red Mexican sash around my waist.
He was a powerful savage, painted red, half-naked,
and held a war-club in his hand.   I clutched tight
around one of his naked legs with both my arms.
He tried to shake me off, but I only clutched the
tighter.   I looked up, and his terrible face almost
froze my blood.   I relaxed my hold from want of
strength.   I shut my eyes, expecting the war-club
to crash through my brain and end the matter at
once, but he only laughed, as much as an Indian
ever allows himself to laugh, and, winding the red
sash around him, strode down the valley.   ·

My pistol was gone.   I crept through the grass
into the stream, then down the stream to where it
nearly touched the forest, and climbed over and
slipped into the wood.

From the timber rim I looked back, but could see
nothing whatever.   The band of horses was gone,

I Relaxed My Hold For Want of Strength.

the Indians had disappeared. All was still. It was truly the stillness of death.

The Indian boys, my companions, had escaped with their ponies into the wood, and I stole up the edge of the forest till I struck their trail, and following on a little way, weak and bewildered, I met them stealing back on foot to my assistance.

My mind and energy both now seemed to give way. We reached the Indian camp somehow, but I have but a vague and shadowy recollection of what passed during the next few weeks. For the most part, as far as I remember, I sat in the lodges or under the trees, or rode a little, but never summoned spirit or energy to return to the fatal camp.

I asked the Indians to go down and see what had become of the two bodies, but they would not. This was quite natural, since they will not revisit their own camp after being driven from it by an enemy, until it is first visited by their priest or medicine man, who chants the death-song and appeases the angered spirit that has brought the calamity upon them. The Indian camp was a small one, and made up mostly of women and children. It was in a vine-maple thicket, on the bend of a small stream.

The camp was but a temporary one, and pitched here for the purpose of gathering and drying a sort of mountain camas root from the low, marshy springs of this region. This camas is a bulbous root shaped much like an onion, and is prepared for food by roasting in the ground, and is very nutritious. Sometimes it is kneaded into cakes and dried. In this state, if kept dry, it will retain its sweetness and fine properties for months.

I could not have been treated more kindly even at home. But Indian life and Indian diet are hardly suited to restore a shattered nervous system and organization so delicate as was my own, and I got on slowly. Perhaps, after all, I only needed rest, and it is quite likely the Indians saw this, for rest I certainly had, such as I never had before or since. It was as near a life of nothingness down there in the deep forest as one well could imagine. There were no birds in the thicket about the camp, and you even had to go out and climb a little hill to get the sun.

This hill sloped off to the south, with the woods open like a park, and here the children and some young women sported noiselessly or basked in the sun.

If there is any place outside of the tomb that

can be stiller than an Indian camp when stillness is required, I do not know where it is. Here was a camp made up mostly of children, and what is usually called the most garrulous half of mankind, and yet all was so still that the deer often walked, stately and unconscious, into our midst.

No mention was made of my going away or remaining. I was permitted, as far as the Indians were concerned, to forget my existence, and so I dreamed along for a month or two, and began to get strong and active in mind and body.

I had dreamed a long dream, and now began to waken and think of active life. I began to hunt and take part with the Indians, and enter into their delights and their sorrows.

Did the world ever stop to consider how an Indian who has no theater, no saloon, no whisky shop, no parties, no newspaper, not one of all our hundreds of ways and means of amusement, spends his evening? Think of this! He is a human being, full of passion and of poetry. His soul must find some expression; his heart some utterance. The long, long nights of darkness, without any lighted city to walk about in, or books to read. Think of that! Well, all this mind, or thought, or soul, or whatever it may be, which we scatter in so many directions, and on so many things, they center on one or two.

What if I told you that they talk more of the future and know more of the unknown than the Christian? That would shock you. Truth is a great galvanic battery.

No wonder they die so bravely, and care so little for this life, when they are so certain of the next.

After a time we moved camp to a less gloomy quarter, and out into the open wood. I now took rides daily or hunted bear or deer with the Indians. Yet, all this time, I had a sort of regretful idea that I must return to the white people and give some account of what had happened. Then I reflected how inglorious a part I had borne, how long I had remained with the Indians, though for no fault of my own, and instinctively knew the virtue of silence on the subject.

In this new camp I seemed to come fully to my strength. I took in the situation and the scenery, and began to observe, to think, and reflect.

Here I found myself alone in an Indian camp without any obligation or anything whatever binding me or calling me back to the Saxon. I began to look on the romantic· side of my life, and was not displeased.

The woods seemed very, very beautiful. The air was so rich, so soft and pure in the Indian summer, that it almost seemed that you could feed upon it. The antlered deer, fat and tame, almost as if fed in parks, stalked by, and game of all kinds filled the woods in herds.

What a fragrance from the long and bent fir boughs. What a healthy breath of pine! All the long sweet moonlight nights the magnificent forest, warm and mellow-like from sunshine gone away, gave out odors like burnt incense from censers swinging in some mighty cathedral.

If I were to look back over the chart of my life for happiness, I should locate it here if anywhere. It is true that there was a little cast of concern in all this about the future, and some remorse for wasted time; and my life, I think, partook of the Indian's melancholy, which comes of solitude and too much thought, but the memory of these few months always appeals to my heart, and strikes me with a peculiar gentleness and uncommon delight.

The Indians were not at war with the whites, nor were they particularly at peace. In fact, they assert that there has never been any peace since they or their fathers can remember. The various tribes, sometimes at war, were also then at peace, so that

nothing whatever occurred to break the calm repose
of the golden autumn.

The mountain streams went foaming down among
the boulders between the leaning walls of yew and
cedar trees toward the Sacramento.   The partridge
whistled and called his flock together when the sun
went down; the brown pheasants rustled as they ran
in strings through the long brown grass, but nothing
else was heard.   The Indians, always silent, are unusually so in autumn.   The majestic march of the
season seemed to make them still.   They moved like
shadows.   The conflicts of civilization were beneath
us.   No sound of strife; the struggle for the possession of usurped lands was far away, and I was glad,
glad as I shall never be again.   I know I should
weary you, to linger here and detail the life we led;
but as for myself I shall never cease to re-live this
life.

With nothing whatever to do but learn their
language and their manners, I made fast progress,
and without any particular purpose at first, I soon
found myself in possession of that which, in the
hands of a man of cunning, would be of great
value.   I saw then how little we know of the Indian.
I had read some flaming picture-books of Indian life,
and I had mixed all my life more or less with the

Indians; that is, such as are willing to mix with us on the border; but the real Indian, the brave, simple, silent and thoughtful Indian who retreats from the white man when he can, and fights when he must, I had never before seen or read a line about. I had never even heard of him. Few have.

A very few years from now the red man, as I found him there in the forests of his fathers, shall not be found anywhere on earth. I am now certain, that, if I had been a man, or even a clever, wide-awake boy, with any particular business with the Indians, I might have spent years in the mountains, and known no more of these people than others know. But, lost as I was, and a dreamer, too ignorant of danger to fear, they sympathized with me, took me into their inner life, told me their traditions.

I began to say to myself, Why cannot they be permitted to remain here? Let this region be untraversed and untouched by the Saxon. Let this be a great National Park, peopled by the Indian only. I saw the justice of this, but did not at that time conceive the possibility of it.

No man leaps full-grown into the world. No great plan bursts into full and complete magnificence and at once upon the mind. Nor does any

one suddenly become this thing or that. A combination of circumstances, a long chain of reverses
that refuses to be broken, carries men far down in
the scale of life, without any fault whatever of
theirs. A similar but less frequent chain of good
fortune lifts others up into the full light of the sun.
Circumstances which few see, and fewer still understand, fashion the destinies of nearly all the active
men of the plastic world. The world watching the
gladiators from its high seat in the circus will
never reverse its thumbs against the successful
man. Therefore succeed, and have the approval
of the world. Nay! what is far better, deserve to
succeed, and have the approval of your own conscience.

CHAPTER V.

THE FINGER-BOARD OF FATE.

I NOW stood face to face with the outposts of the great events of my life. Here were the tawny people with whom I was to mingle. There loomed Mount Shasta, with which my name, if remembered at all, will be remembered.

I visited many of the Indian villages, where I received nothing but kindness and hospitality. They had never before seen so young a white man. The Indian mothers were particularly kind. My tattered clothes were replaced by soft brown buckskins, which they almost forced me to accept. I was not only told that I was welcome, and that they were so glad to see me, but I was made to feel that this was the case. Their men were manly, tall, graceful. Their women were beautiful, and their wild and natural, simple and savage beauty was beyond anything I have since seen, and I have twice gone the circuit of the earth since I first pitched camp at the base of Shasta.

I came to sympathize thoroughly with the Indians. Perhaps, if I had been in a pleasant home,

had friends, or even had the strength of will and
capacity to lay hold of the world, and enter the
conflict successfully, I might have thought much as
others thought, and done as others have done ;
but I was a gypsy, and had no home.   I did not
fear or shun toil, but I despised the treachery and
falsehood practiced in the struggle for wealth, and
kept as well out of it as I could.

All these ideas of mine seem very singular now
for one so young.   Yet it appears to me I always
had them ; maybe, I was born with a nature that
did not fit into the molds of other minds.   At all
events, I began to think very early for myself, and
nearly always as impracticably as possible.   Even at
the time mentioned I had some of the thoughts of
a man ; and at the present time, perhaps, I have
many of the thoughts of a child.   My life on horseback and among herds from the time I was old
enough to ride a horse, had made me even still
more thoughtful and solitary than was my nature,
so that on some things I thought a great deal, or
rather observed, while on other things, practical
things, I never bestowed a moment's time.   I had
never been a boy, that is, an orthodox, old-fash-
ioned boy, for I never played in my life.   Games
of ball, marbles, and the like, are to me still mys-

terious as the rites in a pagan temple. I then knew nothing at all of men. Cattle and horses I understand thoroughly. But somehow I could not understand or get on with my fellow-man. He seemed to always want to cheat me—to get my labor for nothing. I could appreciate and enter into the heart of an Indian. Perhaps it was because he was natural; a child of nature ; nearer to God than the white man. I think what I most needed in order to understand, get on and not be misunderstood, was a long time at school, where my rough points could be ground down. The schoolmaster should have taken me between his thumb and finger and rubbed me about till I was as smooth and as round as the others. Then I should have been put out in the society of other smooth pebbles, and rubbed and ground against them till I got as smooth and pointless as they. You must not have points or anything about you singular or noticeable if you would get on. You must be a pebble, a smooth, quiet pebble. Be a big pebble if you can, a small pebble if you must. But be a pebble just like the rest, cold and hard, and sleek and smooth, and you are all right. But I was as rough as the lava rocks I roamed over,

as broken as the mountains I inhabited; neither a
man nor a boy.

How I am running on about myself, and yet how
pleasant is this forbidden fruit! The world says
you must not talk of yourself. The world is a
tyrant. The world no sooner discovered that the
most delightful of all things was the pleasure of
talking about one's self, even more delightful than
talking about one's neighbor, than straightway the
world, with the wits to back it, pronounced against
the use of this luxury.

Who knows but it is a sort of desire for revenge
against mankind for forbidding us to talk as much
as we like about ourselves, that makes us so turn
upon and talk about our neighbors?

*   *   *   *   *   *   *

Winter was now approaching; and, while I should
have been welcome with the Indians to the end, I
preferred to consider my stay with them in the light
of a visit, and decided to go on to Yreka (a mining
camp then grown to the dignity of a city), and try
my fortune in the mines.

It was unsafe to venture out alone, if not impossible to find the way; but the two young men who
had assisted as vaqueros in the valley set out with
me, and led the way till we touched the trail leading

from Red Bluffs to Yreka, on the eastern spurs of Mount Shasta.   Here they took a tender farewell, turned back, and I never saw them again.

*   *   *   *   *   *   *

I rode down and around the northern end of the deep wood, and down into Shasta Valley.

If I was unfit to take my part in the battle of life when I left home, I was now certainly more so.   My wandering had only made me the more a dreamer. My stay with the Indians had only intensified my dislike for money-makers, and the commercial world in general, and I was as helpless as an Indian.

I was so shy that I only spoke to men when compelled to, and then with the greatest difficulty and embarrassment.   I remember, lonely as I was in my ride to Yreka, that I always took some by-trail, if possible, if about to meet people, in order to avoid them, and at night would camp alone by the wayside, and sleep in my blanket on the ground, rather than come face to face with strangers.

I left the Indians without any intention of returning, whatever.   I had determined to enter the gold mines, dig gold for myself, make a fortune, and return to civilization.

In spite of my resolution to boldly enter the camp or city and bear my part there, as I neared the town

my heart failed me, and I made on to Cottonwood,
a mining camp twenty miles distant, on the Klamat,
and a much smaller town.

After two or three days of unsuccessful attempts
to find some opening, I determined to again marshal
courage and move upon Yreka. I accordingly, on
a clear, frosty morning, mounted my pony, and set
out alone for that place.

I rode down to the banks of the beautiful, arrowy
Klamat — misspelled Klamath — with many peaceful Indians in sight.

A deep, swift stream it was then, beautiful and
blue as the skies; but not so now. The miners
have filled its bed with tailings from the sluice and
tom; they have dumped, and dyked, and mined in
this beautiful river-bed till it flows sullen and turbid
enough. Its Indian name signifies the " giver " or
" generous," from the wealth of salmon it gave the
red men till the white man came to its banks.

The salmon will not ascend the muddy water
from the sea. They come no more, and the red
men are gone.

As I rode down to the narrow river, I saw a tall,
strong gentleman in top boots and silk sash, standing on the banks calling to the ferryman on the
opposite side.

Up to this moment, it seemed to me I had never yet seen a perfect man. This one now before me seemed to leave nothing to be desired in all that goes to make the comely and complete gentlemen. . Young — I should say he was hardly twenty-five — and yet thoroughly thoughtful and in earnest. There was command in his quiet face, and a dignity in his presence, yet a gentleness, too, that won me, and made it seem possible to approach as near his heart as it is well for one man to approach that of another.

This, thought I, as I stood waiting for the boat, is no common person. He is surely a prince in disguise; wild and free, up here in the mountains for pleasure. I associated him with Italian princes dethroned, or even a king of France in exile. He was surely splendid, superb, standing there in the morning sun, in his gay attire, by the swift and shining river, smiling, tapping the sand in an absent-minded sort of way with his boot. A prince! truly nothing less than a prince! The man turned and smiled good-naturedly, as I dismounted, tapped the sand with his top-boot, gently whistled the old air of " '49," but did not speak.

He was attired something after the Mexican style of dress, with a wealth of black hair on his

4

shoulders, a cloak on his arm, and a pistol in his belt.

The boatman came and took us in his narrow little flat, and set his oars for the other side. The handsome stranger spoke to me pleasantly, and I was more than pleased when he accepted my offer to " ride and tie," as we trudged on toward the city together.

It was late in the day when we passed on one side of the dusty road we had been traveling but a short distance, a newly erected gallows; and a populous graveyard on the other. Certain evidences, under the present order of things, of the nearness of civilization.

Mount Shasta is not visible from the city. A long butte, black, and covered with chaparral, lifts up before Yreka, shutting out the presence of the mountain

It was a strange sort of inspiration that made the sheriff come out here to construct his gallows — out in the light, as it were, from behind the little butte, and full in the face of Shasta.

A strange sort of inspiration it was, and more beautiful, that made the miners bring the first dead out here from the camp, from the dark, and dig his grave here on the hillside, full in the light of the lifted and eternal front of snow.

Dead men are even more gregarious than the living. No one lies down to rest long at a time . alone, even in the wildest parts of the Pacific. The dead will come, if his place of rest be not hidden utterly, sooner or later, and even in the wildest places will find him out, and one by one lie down around him.

The shadows of the mountains in mantles of pine were reaching out from the west over the thronged, busy little new-born city, as we entered its populous streets.

The kingly sun, as if it was the last sweet office on earth that day, reached out a shining hand to Shasta, laid it on his head till it became a halo of gold and glory, withdrew it then, and then the shadowy curtains of night came down, and it was dark almost in a moment.

The Prince unfastened his cloak from the machcers behind my saddle, and, as he did so, courteously asked if I was " all right in town," and I boldly answered, " Oh, yes, all right now." Then he bade me good-bye, and walked rapidly up the street.

If I had only had a little nerve, the least bit of

practical common sense and knowledge of men, I
should have answered, " No, sir; I am not all
right at all.   I am quite alone here.   I do not
know a soul in this city or any means of making a
living.   I have nothing in the world but a half-dollar and this pony.   I am tired, cold, hungry, half-
clad, as you see.   No, sir, since you ask me, that
is the plain truth of the matter.   I am not all right
at all."

Had I had the sense or courage to say that, or
any part of that, he would have given me half his
all, and been proud and happy to do it.

I was alone in the mines and mountains of California.   But what was worse than mines and
mountains, I was alone in a city.   I was alone in
the first city I had ever seen.   I could see nothing
here that I had ever seen before, but the cold far
stars above me.

I pretended to be arranging my saddle till the
Prince was out of sight, and then, seeing the sign
of a horse swinging before a stable close at hand, I
led my tired pony there, and asked that he should
be cared for.

CHAPTER VI.

IN A CALIFORNIA MINING CAMP.

I THINK I was ill.   I remember some things but vaguely which took place this night, and the day and night that followed.

I am certain that something was wrong all this time; for, as a rule, when we first land from a voyage, or reach a journey's end, the mind is fresh and strong — a blank ready to receive impressions and to retain them.

If you will observe or recall the fact, you will find that the first city you visited in China, or the first seaport you touched at in Europe, is fixed in your mind more perfectly than any other. But my recollection of this time, usually clear and faultless, is shadowy and indistinct.   I was so weary that I slid down into the manger, under the nose of my pony, and lay there shivering and half doubled up all night.   I was surely ill.

I stole away from the stable at dawn, and reached the main street.   A tide of people poured up and down, and across from other streets, as strong as if in New York.   The white people on the sidewalks, the

Chinese and mules in the main street. Not a
woman in sight, not a child, not a boy. People
turned to look at me as at something new and out
of place.

I was very hungry, faint, miserable. The wind
pitched down from the white-covered mountains,
cold and keen, and whistled above the crowds along
the streets. I got a loaf of bread for my half-dollar,
walked on, ate it unobserved, and was stronger.

I walked up the single long street in that direction,
the hills began to flash back the sun that glowed
from Shasta's helmet, and my heart rose up with
the sun. I said: " The world is before me. Here
is a new world being fashioned under my very feet.
I will take part in the work, and a portion of it
shall be mine."

All this city had been built, all this country
opened up, in less than two years. Twenty months
before, only the Indian inhabited here; he was lord
absolute of the land. But gold had been found on
this spot by a party of roving mountaineers; the
news had gone abroad, and people poured in and
had taken possession in a day, without question and
without ceremony.

And the Indians? They were pushed aside. At
first they were glad to make the strangers welcome;

but, when they saw where it would all lead, they grew sullen and concerned.

I hurried on a mile or so to the foot-hills, and stood in the heart of the placer mines.   Now the smoke from the low chimneys of the log cabins began to rise and curl through the cool, clear air on every hand, and the miners to come out at the low doors; great hairy, bearded, six-foot giants, hatless, and half-dressed.

They stretched themselves in the sweet, frosty air, shouted to each other in a sort of savage banter, washed their hands and faces in the gold-pans that stood by the door, and then entered their cabins again, to partake of the eternal beans and bacon and coffee, and coffee and bacon and beans.

The whole face of the earth was perforated with holes; shafts sunk and being sunk by these men in search of gold, down to the bed-rock.   Windlasses stretched across these shafts, where great buckets swung, in which men hoisted the earth to the light of the sun by sheer force of muscle.

The sun came softly down, and shone brightly on the hillside where I stood.   I lifted my hands to Shasta, above the butte and town, for he looked like an old acquaintance, and again was glad.

It is one of the chiefest delights of extreme

youth, and I may add of extreme ignorance, to
bridge over rivers with a rainbow.   And one of the
chief good things of youth and verdancy is buoy-
ancy of spirits.   You may be twice vanquished in
a day, and, if you are neither old nor wise, you may
still be twice glad.

A sea of human life began to sound and surge
round me.   Strong men shouldered their picks and
shovels, took their gold-pans under their arms, and
went forth to labor.   They sang little snatches of
songs familiar in other lands, and now and then
they shouted back and forth, and their voices arose
like trumpets in the mountain air.

I went down among these men full of hope.   I
asked for work.   They looked at me and smiled,
and went on with their labor.   Sometimes, as I
went from one claim to another, they would ask me
what I could do.   One greasy, red-faced old fellow,
with a green patch over his left eye, a check shirt,
yellow with dirt, and one suspender, asked :

" What in hell are you doing here anyhow ? "

At dusk I again sought the rude, half-open stable,
put my arms around my pony's neck, caressed him
and talked to him as a brother.   I wanted, needed
something to love and talk to, and this horse was
all I had.

Pretty soon the man who kept the stable, a negro, came in and bullied me roundly for having slept in the manger. I waited till he turned away, and then hastened to climb into the loft, and hide ·in a nest of hay.

It was late when I awoke. I had a headache, and hardly knew where I was. When I had collected my mind and understood the situation, I listened for the negro's voice. I heard him in the far part of the stable, and, frightened half to death, hastened to descend.

When a young bear up a tree hears a human voice, it hastens down, even though it be perfectly safe where it is, and will reach the ground only to fall into the very arms of the hunter.

My conduct was something like that of the young bear. I can account for the one about as clearly as for the other.

My hat was smashed in many shapes, my clothes were wrinkled, and there were fragments of hay and straw in my hair. My heart beat audibly, and my head ached till I was nearly blinded with pain as I hastened down.

There was no earthly reason why I should fear this negro. Reason would have told me it was not in his power to harm me; but I had not then grown to use my reason.

There are people who follow instinct and impulse, much as a horse or dog, all through rather eventful lives, and in some things make fewer mistakes than men who act only from reason.

A woman follows instinct more than man does, and hence is keener to detect the good or bad in a face than man, and makes fewer real mistakes.

When I had descended, and turned hastily and half-blinded to the door, there stood the negro, glaring at me ferociously.

" What the holy poker have you been a doin' up there? Stealin' my eggs, eh? Now, look here, you better git. Do you hear?" And he came toward me. "I know you; do you hear? I know you stole dat hoss. Now you git."

What should I do? What did I do? I ran! A boy's legs, like a mule's heels, answer many arguments. They are his last resort, and often his first. Deprive him of everything else, but leave him his legs, and he will get on.

I was not strong. I was not used to making my way through a crowd, and got on slowly. I ran against men coming down the street with picks and pans, and they swore lustily. I ran against China-

men, with great baskets on their bamboo poles,
who took it in good part and said nothing. I
expected every moment this black man would seize
me in his black hands, and lug me off to a prison.
.I was surely delirious.

At last, when near the hotel, I took time to look
over my shoulder. I could see nothing of him;
he perhaps had not left the stable.

As I passed the hotel the Prince came out. He
had slept and rested these two nights, and looked
fresh as the morning.

"How-dy-do?" said the Prince, in his quiet, good-
humored way. "How-dy-do? Take a drink?"
And he led me into the bar-room. I followed
mechanically.

In most parts of America the morning salutation
is, "How d'ye do? How's the folks?" But on the
Pacific it is, "How-dy-do? Take a drink?"

There was a red sign over the door of the hotel
—a miner with a pick, red shirt, and top boots.
I lifted my face and looked at that sign to hide my
expression of concern from the Prince.

"Hullo, my little chicken, what's up? You look
as pale as a ghost. Come, take a smash! It will
strengthen you up. Been on a bender last night;
no?" cried an old sailor, glass in hand.

There was an enormous box-stove there in the
middle of the room, with a drum like a steam boiler
above, and a great wood fire that cracked and roared
like a furnace.

The walls were low, of painted plank, and were
hung around with cheap prints in gay colors — of
race-horses, prize-fighters and bull-dogs.   One end
of the room was devoted to a local picturing, on a
plank half the size of a barn door, which was called
a Mexican Bull.   The great picture of the place,
however, was that of a grizzly bear and hunter,
which hung at the back of the man who dealt out
the tumblers behind the bar.   This picture was
done by the hunter himself.   He was represented
clasped in the bear's embrace, and heroically driving an enormous knife to his heart.   The knife was
big and broad as a handsaw, red and running with
blood.   The bear's forelegs were enormous, and
nearly twice as long and large as his hind ones.
It may be a good stroke of genius to throw all the
strength and power in the points to which the attention will most likely be directed.   At least, that
seemed to be the policy adopted by this artist of the
West.

An Indian scalp or two hung from a corner of this
painting.   The long, matted hair hung streaming

down over the ears of the bear and his red, open mouth. A few sheaves of arrows in quivers were hung against the wall, with here and there a tomahawk, a scalping-knife, boomerang and a war-club, at the back of the " bar-keep."

Little shelves of bottles, glasses and other requisites of a well-regulated bar sprang up on either side of the erect grizzly bear; and on the little shelf where the picture rested lay a brace of pistols, capped and cocked, within hand's reach of the cinnamon-haired barkeeper. This man was short, thick-set, and of enormous strength, strength that had not remained untrained. He had short, red hair, which stuck straight out from the scalp; one tooth out in front, and a long, white scar across his narrow, red forehead. He wore a red shirt, open at the throat, with the sleeves rolled up his brawny arms to the elbows.

All this seems to be before me now. I believe I could count and tell with a tolerable accuracy the number of glasses and bottles there were behind the bar.

Here is something strange. Everything that passed, everything that touched my mind through any source whatever, every form that my eyes rested upon, in those last two or three minutes be-

fore I broke down, remained as fixed and substan-
tial in the memory as shafts of stone.

Is it not because they were the last? because the
mind, in the long blank that followed, had nothing
else to do but fix those last things firmly in their
place, something as the last scene on the land or
the last words of friends are remembered when we
go down on a long journey across the sea?

I have a dim and uncertain recollection of trying
hard to hold on to the bar, of looking up to the
Prince for help in a helpless way; the house seemed
to rock and reel, and then one side of the room was
lifted up so high I could not keep my feet — could
not see distinctly, could not hear at all, and then
all seemed to recede; and all the senses refused to
struggle longer against the black and the blank sea
that came over me, and all things around me.

The Prince, I think, put out his strong arms and
took me up, but I do not know.   All this is painful to recall.   I never asked anything about it when
I got up again, because I tried to forget it.   That
is impossible.   I see that bar, barkeeper, and
grizzly bear so distinctly this moment, that, if I were
a painter, I could put every face, every tumbler,
everything there, on canvas as truthfully as they
could be taken by a photograph.

CHAPTER VII.

DOWN AMONG THE DEAD.

A CHANGE had suddenly come over the actions, and, I may say, the mind of the Prince. He saw that I was alone, friendless, helpless. He put out his hand and drew me to his heart. He made me his own. I had fallen into his hands so helplessly and so wholly that I was in a way absolutely his. He did not shift the responsibility, nor attempt to escape it.

I could not, of course, then understand why my presence, or the responsibility of a young person thrown on him in this way, could have influenced him for good or evil, or have altered his plans or course of life in any way at all. I think I can now. I did not stop to inquire then. It so happens that when very young we are not particular about reasons for anything.

It is often a fortunate thing for a man that the fates have laid some responsibility to his charge. From what I could learn the Prince was utterly alone; had no one depending on him; had formed no very ardent attachments; expected, of course,

to leave the mountains sometime, and settle down
as all others were doing, but did not just then care
to fix the time, or assume any concern about it.

Naturally noble and generous in all his instincts,
he fell to planning first for me, and then for himself
and me together. He saw no prospect better than
that of an honest miner. For, be it known, this
man was, or had been, a gambler.

After casting about for many days in the
various neighboring localities, the Prince finally
decided to pitch his tent on a tributary of the
Klamat, and the most flourishing, newly discovered
camp of the north. It lay west of the city, a day's
ride down in a deep, densely timbered cañon, out of
sight of Mount Shasta, out of sight of everything —
even the sun; save here and there where a land-
slide had plowed up the forest, or the miners had
mown down the great evergreens about their cabins, or town sites in the camp.

I asked the Prince to go down and see about my
pony when we were about to set out, but the negro
had confiscated him long since — claimed to have
disposed of him for his keeping. " He's eat his
cussed head off," said he, and I saw my swift, patient
little companion no more.

On a crisp morning, we set out from the city,

and, when we had reached the foot-hills to the west, we struck a fall of snow, with enormous hare, ears as large, almost, as those of Mexican mules, crossing here and there, and coyotes sitting on the ground, tame as dogs, looking down on the cabins and camp below.

We had, strapped to our saddles behind us, blankets, picks, shovels, frying-pans, beans, bacon and coffee,—all, of course, in limited quantities.

The two mules snuffed at the snow, lifted their little feet gingerly, spun around many times like tops, and brayed a solemn prayer or two to be allowed to turn back.

Snow is a mule's aversion. Give him sand, even the heat of a furnace, and only sage-brush to subsist upon, and he will go on patient and uncomplaining; but snow goes against his nature. We began to leave the world below—the camps, the clouds of smoke, and the rich smell of the burning juniper and manzanita.

The pines were open on this side of the mountain, so that sometimes we could see through the trees to the world without and below. Over against us stood Shasta. Grander, nearer, now he seemed than ever, covered with snow from base to crown.

5

If you would see any mountain in its glory, you must go up a neighboring mountain, and see it above the forests and lesser heights. You must see a mountain with the clouds below you and between you and the object of contemplation.

Until you have seen a mountain over the tops and crests of a sea of clouds, you have not seen, and cannot understand, the sublime and majestic scenery of the Pacific.

Never, until on some day of storms in the lower world you have ascended one mountain, looked out above the clouds, and seen the white, snowy pyramids piercing here and there the rolling, nebulous sea, can you hope to learn the freemasonry of mountain scenery in its grandest, highest and most supreme degree. Lightning and storms and thunder underneath you; calm and peace and perfect beauty about you. Typical and suggestive.

Sugar-pines, tall as pyramids, on either hand as we rode up the trail, through the dry, bright snow, with great burs or cones, long as your arm, swaying from the tips of their lofty branches ; and little pine squirrels, black and brown, ran up and down busy with their winter hoard.

Once on the summit, we dismounted, drew the cinches till the mules grunted and put in a protest with their teeth and heels, and then began the descent.

The Prince had been silent all day, but, as we were mounting the mules again, he said :

" We may have a rocky time down there, my boy. The grass is mighty short with me, I tell you. But I have thought it all out, clean down to the bed-rock, and this is the best that can be done. If we can manage to scratch through this winter, we will be all right for a big clean-up by the time snows fly over again ; and then, if you like, you shall see another land. There ! look down there," he said, as we came to the rim of a bench in the mountain, and had a look-out below, " that is the place where we shall winter. Three thousand people there ! not a woman, not a child ! Two miles below, and ten miles ahead ! "

Not a woman ? Not much of a chance for a love affair. He who consents to descend with me into the deep, dark gorge in the mountains, and live the weary winter through, will see neither the light of the sun, nor the smiles of woman. A sort of Hades. A savage Eden, with many Adams walking up and down, and plucking of every tree, nothing forbidden here; for here, so far as it would seem, are neither laws of God or man.

When shall we lie down and sleep, and awake and find an Eve and the Eden in the forest ? — an Eve untouched and unstained, fresh from the hand of God, gazing at her reflection in the mossy mountain stream, amazed at her beauty, and in love with herself; even in this first act setting an example for man that he has followed too well for his own peace.

This cañon was as black as Erebus down there — a sea of somber firs; and down, down as if the earth was cracked and cleft almost in two. Here and there lay little nests of clouds below us, tangled in the treetops, no wind to drive them, nothing to fret and disturb. They lay above the dusk of the forest as if asleep. Over across the cañon stood another mountain, not so fierce as this, but black with forest, and cut and broken into many gorges — scars of earthquake shocks, and saber-cuts of time. Gorge on gorge, cañon intersecting cañon, pitching down toward the rapid Klamat — a black and boundless forest till it touches the very tide of the sea a hundred miles to the west.

Our cabin was on the mountain side. Where else could it have been but on the mountain top? Nothing but mountains. A little stream went creeping down below — a little wanderer among the boulders — for it was now sorely fretted and roiled by the thousands of miners up and down.

There was a town, a sort of common center, called The Forks; for here three little streams joined hands, and went down from there to the Klamat together. Our cabin stood down on the main stream, not far from the river.

The principal saloon of The Forks was the " Howlin' Wilderness;" an immense pine-log cabin, with higher walls than most cabins, earth floor, and an immense fire-place, where crackled and roared, day and night, a pine-log fire that filled the place with perfume and warmth.

There was a tall man, a sort of half sport and half miner, who had a cabin close to town, who seemed to take a special interest in this place. He was known as " Long Dan," always carried two pistols, and took a pride in getting into trouble.

" Look here," said Prince, to him one evening, after he had been telling his six-shooter adventures, with great delight, by the cabin fire, " Look here, Dan, some of these days you will die with your boots on. Now, see if you don't; if you keep on slinging your six-shooter around loose in this sort of a way, you will go up the flume as slick as a salmon — die with your boots on before you know it."

Dan smiled blandly as he tapped an ivory pistol-butt, and said, " Bet you the cigars I don't! Whenever my man comes to the center, I will call him, see if I don't, and get away with it too."

Now, to understand the pith of the grim joke which Dan played in the last act, you must know that " dying with the boots on "means a great deal in the mines.   It is the poetical way of expressing the result of a bar-room or street battle.

Let me here state, that, while the wild, semi-savage life of the mines and mountains has brought forth no dialect to speak of, it has produced many forms of expression that are to be found nowhere else.

These sharp sword-cuts are sometimes coarse, sometimes wicked, but always forcible, and driven to the hilt.   They are even sometimes strangely poetical, and, when you know their origin, they carry with them a touch of tenderness beyond the reach of song.

Take, for example, the last words of the old Sierra Nevada stage-driver, who, for a dozen years, had sat up on his box in storm and sun, and dashed down the rocky roads, with his hat on his nose, his foot on the brake, and the four lines threaded through his fingers.   '

The old hero of many encounters with robbers and floods and avalanches in the Sierras, was dying now. His friends gathered around him to say fare-well. He half raised his head, lifted his hands as if still at his post, and said:

" Boys, I am on the down grade, and can't reach the brake!" and sank down and died.

And so it is that " the down grade," an expression born of the death of the old stage-driver, has a meaning with us now.

A Saturday or so after the conversation alluded to between Long Dan and the Prince, there were heard pistol-shots in the direction of the Howlin' Wilderness saloon, and most of the men rushed forth to see what Jonah, fate had pitched upon to be thrown into the sea of eternity, and be the " man for breakfast " this time.

Nothing " draws " like a bar-room fight of California. It is a sudden thing. Sharp and quick come the keen reports, and the affair has the advantage of being quite over by the time you reach the spot, and all danger of serving the place of barricades for a stray bullet is past.

I have known miners standing on their good

behavior, who resisted the temptations of hurdy-
gurdy houses, bull-fights, and bull and bear encounters, who always wrote home on Sundays,
read old letters, and said the Lord's prayer; but I
never yet knew one who could help going to see
the dead man, or the scene of the six-shooter war-
dance, whenever the shots were heard.

The Prince rushed up. The house was full; surging and excited men with their hats knocked off,
their faces red with passion, and their open red
shirts showing their strong, hairy bosoms.

" It is Long Dan," some one called out; and this
made the Prince, who was his neighbor, push his
way more eagerly through the men. He reached
the wounded man at last, and the crowd, who knew
the Prince as an acquaintance of the sufferer, fell
back and gave him a place at his side.

The proprietors of the Howlin' Wilderness had
set up the monte table, which had been overthrown
in the struggle, and laid the dying Dan gently there
with an old soldier overcoat under his head.

When the Prince took up the helpless hand of
the poor fellow, so overthrown in his pride and
strength, and spoke to him, he slowly opened his
eyes, looked straight at the Prince with a smile,
only perceptible, hardly as distinct as the tear in

"Prince, Prince, Old Boy, I've Won the Cigars."

his eye, and said, in a whisper, as he drew the Prince down to his face:

"Old fellow, Prince, old boy, take off my boots."

The Prince hastened to obey, and again took his place at his side.

Again Long Dan drew him down, and said, huskily:

"Prince, Prince, old boy, I've won the cigars! I've won 'em, by the holy poker!"

And so he died.

CHAPTER VIII.

SNOW! NOTHING BUT SNOW!

SUCH fearful scenes were the chief diversions of the camp. True, the miners did not, as a rule, take part in these bloody carnivals, but were rather the spectators in the circus. The men at The Forks, gamblers and the like, were the gladiators.

Of course, we had some few papers, very old ones, and there were some few novels on the creek; but there was no place of amusement, no neighbors with entertaining families, nothing but the monotony of camp and cabin life of the most ungracious kind.

We had a claim down among the boulders, boulders as big as a barn, at the base of the cabin, in the creek; but, if it contained any gold worth mentioning, we had not yet had any real evidence of it.

We toiled — let that be understood — we two together. I, of course, was not strong, and not worth much; but he, from dawn till dark, never took rest at all. He was in earnest — thoughtful man now.

He was working on a new problem, and was concerned. Often at night, by the light of the pine-
log fire, I would see the severe lines of thought
across his splendid face, and wished that I, too, was
a strong man, and such a man as this.

It was a severe and cruel winter. I remember one
Sunday I went down to the claim and found a lot
of Californian quails frozen to death in the snow.
They had huddled up close as possible; tried to keep
warm, but perished there, every one. Maybe this
was because we had cut away all the underbrush
up and down the creek, and let in the cold and snow,
and left the birds without a shelter.

The Prince was entirely without money now, and
anything in the shape of food was fifty cents and a
dollar a pound. It was a great fall from his grand life
the year before. It remained to be seen if he would
be consumed in the fire, or would come out only
brightened and beautified.

The cold weather grew sharply colder. One
morning when I arose and went down to the stream
to wash my hands and face, and snuff the keen,
crisp air, the rushing mountain stream was still;
not even the plunge and gurgle underneath the
ice. It was frozen stiff, and laid out in a long white
shroud of frost and ice, and fairy-work by delicate

hands, was done all along the border; but the stream was still — dead, utterly dead.

The strip of sky that was visible above us grew dark and leaden. Some birds flew frightened past, crossing the cañon above our heads and seeking shelter; and squirrels ran up and down the pines and frozen hillsides in silence and in haste. We instinctively, like the birds, began to prepare for the storm, and stored in wood all day till a whole corner of the cabin was filled with logs of pine and fir, sweet-smelling juniper and manzanita to kindle with, and some splinters of pitch, riven from a sugar pine seamed and torn by lightning, up the hill.

The Prince kept hard at work, patient and cheerful all day, but still he was silent and thoughtful. I did not ask him any questions; I trusted this man, loved him, leaned on him, believed in him solely. It was strange, and yet not strange, considering my fervid, passionate nature, my inexperience, and utter ignorance of men and things. But he was worthy. I had never seen a full, splendid, sincere, strong man like this. I had to have some one —something — to love; it was a necessity of my nature. This man answered all, and I was satisfied. Had he called me some morning and said, " Come, we will start north now, through this snow;" or, " Come, let us go to the top of Mount Shasta, and warm us by the furnace of the volcano there," I had not hesitated a moment, never questioned the wisdom and propriety of the journey, but followed him with the most perfect faith and undoubting zeal and energy.

The next morning there was a bank of snow against the door when I opened it. The trail was level and obliterated, Snow! snow! snow! The stream that had lain all day in state, in its shroud of frost and fairy-work, was buried now, and beside the grave, the elder and yew along the bank bent their heads and drooped their limbs in sad and beautiful regret ; a patient, silent sorrow.

Over across from the cabin the mountain side shot up at an angle almost frightful to look upon, till it lost its pine-covered summit in the clouds, and lay now a slanting sheet of snow.

The trees had surrendered to the snow. They no longer shook their sable plumes, or tossed their heads at all. Their limbs reached out no more triumphant in the storm, but drooped and hung in silence at their sides — quiet, patient, orderly as soldiers in a line, with grounded arms. Back of us the same scene was lifted to the clouds.

Snow! snow! snow! nothing but snow! To right and to left, up and down the buried stream, were cabins covered with snow, white and cold as tombs and stones of marble in a churchyard.

And still the snow came down steadily and white, in flakes like feathers. It did not blow or bluster about as if it wanted to assert itself. It seemed as if it already had absolute control; rather like a king, who knows that all must and will bow down before him.

Steady and still, strong and stealthy, it came upon us and possessed the earth. Not even a bird was heard to chirp, or a squirrel to chatter a protest now. High over head, in the clouds as it seemed, or rather back of us a little, on the steep and stupendous mountain, it is true a coyote lifted his nose to the snow, and called out dolefully; but that, may be, was a call to his mate across the cañon, in the clouds on the hill-top opposite. That was all that could be heard.

The trail was blocked, and the butcher came no more. This was a sad thing to us. I know that more than once that morning the Prince went to the door and looked up sharply toward the point where the mule made his appearance when the trail was open, and that his face expressed uncommon concern when he had settled in his mind that the beef supply was at an end.

It is pretty certain that the two butchers had been waiting for some good excuse to shut up shop without offending the miners, until their claims should be opened in the spring. This they now had, and at once took advantage of the opportunity.

We could mine no more, could pick-and-shovel no more, with frosty fingers, in the frozen ground, by the pine-log fire, down by the complaining, troubled little stream. The mine was buried with the brook.

That stream had never seemed satisfied before. It ran, and foamed, and fretted, hurried and hid under the boughs and bushes, held onto the roots and grasses, and lifted little white hands as it ran toward the Klamat, a stronger and braver brother, as if there were grizzlies up the gorge where it came from. At best, it had but a sorry time, even before the miners came. It had to wedge itself in between the foot-hills, and elbow its way for every inch of room. It was kicked and cudgeled from this foot-hill to that; it ran from side to side, and worked, and wound, and curved, and cork-screwed on in a way that had made an angler sorry. Maybe, after all, it was glad to fold its little icy hands across its fretted breast, and rest, and rest, and rest, stiff and still, beneath the snow, below the pines and yew and cedar trees that bent their heads in silence by the sleeper. Certainly it was satisfied now.

The Kanaka sugar-mat was empty; the strip of bacon that had hung in the corner against the wall was gone, and the flour-sack grew low and suggestive.

Miners are great eaters in the winter. Snuff the fierce frost weather of the Sierras, run in the snow, or delve in the mine through the day, and roast by a great pine fire through the evening, and you will eat like an Englishman.

The snow had fallen very fast; then the weather settled cold and clear as a bell. The largest and the brightest stars, it seemed to me, hang about and above Mount Shasta in those cold, bright winter nights of the north. They seem as large as California lilies; they flash and flare, and sparkle and dart their little spangles; they lessen and enlarge, and seem to make signs, and talk and understand each other, in their beautiful blue home, that seems in the winter time so near the summit of the mountain blazing on this awful altar eternally to the Eternal.

The Indians say that it is quite possible to step from this mountain to the stars. They say that their fathers have done so often. They lay so many great achievements to their fathers. In this they are very like the white man. But maybe, after all, some of their fathers have gone from this mountain-top to the stars. Who knows?

We could do nothing but get wood, cook, and eat. It did not take us long to cook and eat.

The bill of fare was short enough. Miners nearly always lay in a great store of provisions — enough to last them through all the winter, as no stores or supply posts are kept open when the mines are closed, as they were then. With us that was impossible. All the others up and down the stream, with few exceptions, had complete supplies on hand, and had a good and jovial time generally.

They got wood, made snow-shoes, cleared off race tracks, and ran races by hundreds on great shoes, twelve and fifteen feet in length, or made coasting places on the hillsides, and slid down hill.

At night, many would get out the old greasy pack of cards, sit before the fire and play innocent games of old sledge, draw poker, euchre or whist, while some would read by the pine-log light. Others, possessed with a little more devilment or restless-

6

ness, maybe, or idle curiosity, would take the single deep-cut trail that led to The Forks, and bring up down at the crackling fire-place of the Howlin' Wilderness.

One morning we had only bread for breakfast. The Prince was gloomy and silent as we sat down. He did not remain long at the table. He arose and stood by the fire, and watched my relish of the little breakfast with evident satisfaction.

"Little one," said he, at last, "it is getting mighty rocky. I tell you, the grass is shorter than it ever was with us before, and what to do next I do not know."

There was something affecting in the voice and manner. My breakfast was nearly choking me, and I tried to hide my face from his. I got up from the table, went to the door and looked across into the white sheet of snow hung upon the mountain opposite, got the air, came back, kicked the fire vigorously, and turned and stood by his side with my back to the fire also.

The weather was still clear and cold. There was, of course, no absolute need of going hungry there, as far as we two were concerned, if we had had the courage, or, rather, the cowardice, to **ask** for bread.

But this man was a proud man, and a complete man, I take it; and, when a man of that nature gets cornered, he is going to endure a great deal before he makes any sign.   A true man can fight, he can kill, but he cannot ask for quarter.   Want only makes such a man more sensitive.   Distress only intensifies his proud and passionate nature, and he prepares himself for everything possible but an appeal to man. Besides, this man was not altogether a miner.   He had never felt that he had won his place among the brawny, broad-shouldered men, who from the first, and all through life, had borne and accepted the common curse that fell on man through the first transgression, and he had always held himself somewhat aloof.

Perhaps he was fighting a battle with himself. Who knows?   It seems to me now, although I had no thought of such a thing then, that he had made a resolve within himself to make his bread by the sweat of his brow, to set a good example to one whom fate had given into his charge, and never turn back or deviate from the one direction.

What that man must have felt would be painful to consider.   As for myself, I did not take in all the situation, or really half of it.   This man, somehow, stood to me like a tower.   I had no fear.

The weather was still intensely cold.   That afternoon the Prince said:

"Come, we will go to town."

CHAPTER IX.

BLOOD ON THE SNOW.

THERE was a tribe of Indians camped down on the rapid, rocky Klamat River — a sullen, ugly set were they, too: at least so said The Forks. Never social, hardly seeming to notice the whites, who were now thick about them, below them, above them, on the river all around them. Sometimes we would meet one on the narrow trail; he would gather his skins about him, hide his bow and arrows under their folds, and, without seeming to see any one, would move past us still as a shadow. I do not remember that I ever saw one of these Indians laugh, not even to smile. A hard-featured, half-starved set of savages, of whom the wise men of the camp prophesied no good.

The snow, unusually deep this winter, had driven them all down from the mountains, and they were compelled to camp on the river.

The game, too, had been driven down along with the Indians, but it was of but little use to them. Their bows and arrows did poor competition with the rifles of the whites in the killing of the game.

The whites had fairly filled the cabins with deer
and elk in their season, got the lion's share, and
left the Indians almost destitute.

Another thing that made it rather more hard on
the Indians than anything else, was the utter failure of the annual run of salmon the summer before,
on account of the muddy water. The Klamat,
which had poured from the mountain lakes to the
sea as clear as glass, was now made muddy and
turbid from the miners washing for gold on its
banks and tributaries. The trout turned on their
sides and died; the salmon from the sea came in
but rarely on account of this; and what few did
come were pretty safe from the spears of the
Indians, because of the colored water; so that the
supply, which was more than all others their bread
and their meat, was entirely cut off.

Mine? It was all a mystery to these Indians as
long as they were permitted to live. I have seen
them gather in groups on the bank above the mines
and watch in silence for hours as if endeavoring to
make it out; they would shrug their shoulders,
draw their skins closer about them, and stalk away
no wiser than before.

Why we should tear up the earth, toil like
gnomes from sun-up to sun-down, rain or sun,

destroy the forests and pollute the rivers, was to them more than a mystery—it was a terror. I believe they accepted it as a curse, the work of evil spirits, and so bowed to it in sublime silence.

This loss of salmon was a greater loss than you would suppose. These fish in the springtime pour up these streams from the sea in incalculable schools. They fairly darken the water. On the head of the Sacramento, before that once beautiful river was changed from a silver sheet to a dirty yellow stream, I have seen between the Devil's Castle and Mount Shasta the stream so filled with salmon that it was impossible to force a horse across the current. Of course, this was not usual, and now can only be met with hard up at the heads of mountain streams where mining is not carried on, and where the advance of the fish is checked by falls on the head of the stream. The amount of salmon which the Indians would spear and dry in the sun, and hoard away for winter. under such circumstances, can be imagined.

What made matters worse, there was a set of men, low men, of the lowest type, who would hang around those lodges at night, give the Indians whisky of the vilest sort, debauch their women, and cheat the men out of their skins and bows and arrows.

Perhaps there was a grim sort of philosophy in
the red man so disposing of his bows and arrows
now that the game was gone and they were of no
further use.   Sold them for bread for his starving
babes, maybe.   How many tragedies are hidden
here?   How many tales of devotion, self-denial,
and sacrifice, as true as the white man ever lived,
as pure, and brave, and beautiful as ever gave
tongue to eloquence or pen to song, sleep here
with the dust of these sad and silent people on the
bank of the stormy river!

In this condition of things, about mid-winter,
when the snow was deep and crusted stiff, and all
nature seemed dead and buried in a ruffled shroud,
there was a murder.   The Indians had broken out!
The prophesied massacre had begun!

Killed by the Indians!   It swept like a telegram
through the camp.   Confused and incoherent, it is
true, but it gathered force and form as the tale flew
on from tongue to tongue, until it assumed a frightful shape.

A man had been killed by the Indians down at
the rancheria.   Not much of a man, it is true.

Killed, too, down in the Indian camp when he
should have been in bed, or at home, or at least in
company with his kind.

All this made the miners hesitate a bit as they hurriedly gathered in at The Forks, with their long Kentucky rifles, their pistols capped and primed, and bowie-knives in their belts.

But as the gathering storm that was to sweep the Indians from the earth took shape and form, these honest men stood out in little knots, leaning on their rifles in the streets, and gravely questioned whether, all things considered, the death of the " Chicken," for that was the dead man's name, was sufficient cause for interference.

To their eternal credit these men mainly decided that it was not, and two by two they turned away, went back to their cabins, hung their rifles up on the rack, and turned their thoughts to their own affairs.

But the hangers-on about the town were terribly enraged. " A man has been killed! " they proclaimed aloud. " A man has been murdered by the savages!! We shall all be massacred! butchered! burnt!! "

In one of the saloons where men were wont to meet at night, have stag-dances, and drink lightening, a short, important man, with the print of a glass-tumbler cut above his eye, arose and made a speech.

" Fellow-miners [he had never touched a pick in his life], I am ready to die for me counthry! [He was an Irishman sent out to Sydney at the Crown's expense.] What have I to live for? [Nothing whatever, as far as any one could tell.] Fellow-miners, a man has been kilt by the treacherous savages — kilt in cold blood! Fellow-miners, let us advance upon the inemy. Let us — let us — fellow-miners, let us take a drink and advance upon the inemy."

" Range around me. Rally to the bar and take a drink, every man of you, at me own ixpense."

The barkeeper, who was also proprietor of the place, a man not much above the type of the speaker, ventured a mild remonstrance at this whole-sale generosity; but the pistol, flourished in a very suggestive way, settled the matter, and, with some · thing of a groan, he set his decanters to the crowd, and became a bankrupt.

This was the beginning; they passed from saloon to saloon, or, rather, from door to door; the short, stout Irishman making speeches, and the mob gathering force and arms as it went, and then, wild with drink and excitement, moved down upon the Indians, some miles away on the bank of the river.

" Come," said the Prince to me, as they passed

out of town, " let us see this through. Here will be
blood. We will see from the hill overlooking the
camp. I hope the Indians are armed — hope to
God they are ' heeled,' and that they will receive
the wretches warmly as they deserve."

Maybe his own wretchedness had something to
do with his wrath; but I think not. I should rather
say that, had he been in strength and spirits, and
had his pistols, which had long since been disposed
of for bread, he had met this mob face to face, and
sent it back to town.

We followed not far behind the crowd of fifty or
sixty men armed with pistols, rifles, knives, and
hatchets.

The trail led to a little point overlooking the bar
on which the Indian huts were huddled.

The river made a bend about there. It ground
and boiled in a crescent blocked with running
ice and snow. The Indians were out in the extreme curve of a horse-shoe made by the river, and
we advanced from without. They were in a net.
They had only a choice of deaths ; death by drown-
ing, or death at the hands of their hereditary foe.

It was nearly night ; cold and sharp the wind
blew up the river, and the snow flew around like
feathers. Not an Indian to be seen. The thin

blue smoke came slowly up, as if afraid to leave
the wigwams, and the traditional, ever-watchful
and wakeful Indian dog was not to be seen or
heard. The men hurried down upon the camp,
spreading out upon the horse-shoe as they ac-
vanced in a run.

" Stop here," said the Prince ; and we stood from
the wind behind a boulder that stood, tall as a
cabin, upon the bar. The crowd advanced to
within half a pistol shot, and gave a shout as they
drew and leveled their arms. Old squaws came
out — bang! bang! bang! shot after shot, and they
were pierced and fell, or turned to run.

The whites, yelling, howling, screaming, were
now among the lodges, shooting down at arm's
length man, woman, or child. Some attempted
the river, I should say, for I afterward saw streams
of blood upon the ice, but not one escaped ; nor
was a hand raised in defense. It was all done in
a little time. Instantly, as the shots and shouts
began, we two advanced, we rushed into the camp,
and, when we reached the spot, only now and then
a shot was heard within a lodge, dispatching a
wounded man or woman.

The few surviving children — for nearly all had
been starved to death — had taken refuge under

skins and under lodges overthrown, hidden away as little kittens will hide just old enough to spit and hiss, and hide when they first see the face of man. These were now dragged forth and shot. Not all these men who made this mob, bad as they were, did this — only a few ; but enough to leave, as far as they could, no living thing.

The babies did not scream. Not a wail, not a sound. The murdered men and women, in the few minutes that the breath took leave, did not even groan.

As we came up a man named " Shon " — at least, that was all the name I knew for him — held up a baby by the leg, a naked, bony little thing, which he had dragged from under a lodge — held it up with one hand, and with the other blew its head to pieces with his pistol.

I must stop here to say that this man Shon soon left camp, and was afterward hung by the Vigilance Committee near Lewiston, Idaho Territory; that he whined for his life like a puppy, and he died like a coward as he was. I chronicle this fact with a feeling of delight.

He was a tall, spare man, with small, gray eyes, a weak, wicked mouth, colorless and treacherous, that was forever smiling and smirking in your face.

Shun a man like that.   A man who always smiles
is a treacherous-natured coward.

He knows, himself, how villainous and contempt-
ible he is, and he feels that you know it too, and so
tries to smile his way into your favor.   Turn away
from that man who smiles and smiles, and rubs his
hands as if he felt, and all men knew, that they
were really dirty.

You can put more souls of such men as that
inside of a single grain of sand than there are dimes
in the national debt.

This man threw down the body of the child
among the dead, and rushed across to where a pair
of ruffians had dragged up another, a little girl,
naked, bony, thin as a shadow, starved into a ghost.
He caught her by the hair with a howl of delight,
placed the pistol to her head, and turned around to
point the muzzle out of range of his companions
who stood around on the other side.

The child did not cry — she did not even flinch.
Perhaps she did not know what it meant; but I
should rather believe she had seen so much of death
there, so much misery, the steady, silent work of
the monster famine through the village day after
day that she did not care.   I saw her face; it did

not even wince. Her lips were thin and fixed, and firm as iron.

The villain, having turned her around, now lifted his arm, cocked the pistol, and —

" Stop that! Stop that, or die! You damned assassin, let go that child, or I will pitch you neck and crop into the Klamat."

The Prince had him by the throat with one hand, and with the other he wrested the pistol from his grasp and threw it into the river. The Prince had not even so much as a knife. The man did not know this, nor did the Prince care, or he had not thrown away the weapon he wrung from his hand. The Prince pushed the child behind him, and advanced toward the short, fat Sydney convict, who had turned, pistol in hand, in his direction.

" Keep your distance, or I will send you to hell across lots in a second."

The man turned away cowed and baffled. He had looked in the Prince's face, and seen his master.

As for myself, I was not only helpless, but, as was always the case on similar occasions, stupid, awkward, speechless. I went up to the little girl, however, got a robe out of one of the lodges — for they had not yet set fire to the village — and put it around her naked little body. After that, as I moved about among the dead, or stepped aside to the river to see the streams of blood on the snow and ice, she followed close as a shadow behind me, but said nothing.

Suddenly there was a sharp yell, a volley of oaths, exclamations, a scuffle, and blows.

" Scalp him! Scalp him! the little savage! Scalp him and throw him in the river! "

From out of the piles of dead somewhere, no one could tell exactly where or when, an apparition had sprung up — a naked little Indian boy, that might have been all the way from twelve to twenty, armed with a knotted war-club, and had fallen upon his foes like a fury.

The poor little hero, starved into a shadow, stood little show there, though he had been a very Hercules in courage. He was felled almost instantly by kicks and blows; and the very number of his enemies saved his life, for they could neither shoot nor stab him with safety, as they crowded and crushed around him.

How or why he was finally spared, was always a marvel. Quite likely the example of the Prince had moved some of the men to more humanity.

When the crowd that had formed a knot about

him had broken up, and I first got sight of him, he was sitting on a stone with his hands between his naked legs, and blood dripping from his long hair, which fell down in strings over his forehead. He had been stunned by a grazing shot, no doubt, and had fallen among the first. He came up to his work, though, like a man, when his senses returned, and, without counting the chances, lifted his two hands to do with all his might the thing he had been taught.

Valor, such valor as that, is not a cheap or common thing. It is rare enough to be respected even by the worst of men. It is only the coward who affects to despise such courage.

This boy sat there on the stone as the village burned, the smoke from burning skins, the wild-rye straw, willow-baskets and Indian robes, ascended, and a smell of burning bodies went up to the Indians' God and the God of us all, and no one said nay, and no one approached him; the men looked at him from under their slouched hats as they moved around, but said nothing.

I pitied him. God knows I pitied him. I was a boy myself, alone, helpless, in an army of strong and unsympathetic men. I would have gone up and put my arms about the wild and splendid little

7

savage, bloody and desperate as he was, so lonely now, so intimate with death, so pitiful! if I had dared, dared the reproach of men-brutes.

There was a sort of nobility about him; his recklessness, his desire to die, lifting his little arms against an army of strong and reckless men, his proud and defiant courage, that made me feel at once that he was above me, stronger, somehow better, than I. Still, he was a boy, and I was a boy —the only boys in the camp, and my heart went out, strong and true, toward him.

The work of destruction was now too complete. There was not found another living thing — nothing but two or three Indians that had been shot and shot, and yet seemed determined never to die, that lay in the bloody snow down toward the rim of the river.

Naked nearly, they were, and only skeletons, with the longest and blackest hair tangled and tossed, and blown in strips and strings, or in clouds out on the white and the blood-red snow, or down their tawny backs, or over their bony breasts, about their dusky forms, fierce and unconquered, with the bloodless lips set close, and blue, and cold, and firm, like steel.

The dead lay around us, piled up in places, limbs

twisted with limbs in the wrestle with death; a mother embracing her boy here; an arm thrown around a neck there; as if these wild people could love as well as die.

In the village, some of the white men claimed to have found something that had been stolen. I have no idea there is any truth in it. I wish there was; then there might be some shadow of excuse for all the murders that made up this cruel tragedy, all of which is, I believe, literally true; truer than nine-tenths of the history and official reports written, wherein these people are mentioned; and I stand ready to give names, dates, and detail to all whom it may concern.

Let me not here be misunderstood. An Indian is no better than a white man. If he sins let him suffer. But I do protest against this custom of making up a case—this custom of deciding the case against him in favor of the white man, forever, on the evidence of the white man only; even though that custom be, in the language of the law, so old " that the memory of man runneth not to the contrary."

The white man and red man are much alike, with one great difference. which you must and will set down to the advantage of the latter.

The Indian has no desire for fortune ; he has no wish in his wild state to accumulate wealth ; and it is in his wild state that he must be judged, for it is in this condition that he is said to sin.   If " money is the root of all evil," as Solomon hath it, then the Indian has not that evil, or that root of evil, or any desire for it.

It is the white man's monopoly.   If an Indian loves you, trusts you, or believes in you at all, he will serve you, guide you through the country, fol-low you to battle, fight for you, he and all his sons and kindred, and never think of the pay or profit. He would despise it if offered, beyond some pres-ents, some tokens of remembrance, decorations, or simplest articles of use.

Again, I do vehemently protest against taking the testimony of border Indians or any Indians with whom the white man comes in constant con-tact, and to whom he has taught the use of money and the art of lying.

And most particularly I do protest against taking these Indians — renegades — who affiliate, mix and strike hands with the whites, as representative Indians.   Better take our own " camp followers " as respectable and representative soldiers.

When you reflect that for centuries the Indians

in almost every lodge on the continent, at almost
every council, have talked of the whites and their
aggressions, and of these things chiefly, and always
with that bitterness which characterizes people who
look at and see only one side of the case, then you
may come to understand, a little, their eternal
hatred of their hereditary enemy — how deeply
seated this is, how it has become a part of their
nature, and, above all, how low, fallen, and how
unlike a true Indian one must be who leaves his
retreating tribe and lingers in a drunken and
debauched fellowship with the whites, losing all
his virtues, and taking on all the vices of his
enemy.

The true Indian retires before the white man's
face to the forest and to the mountain tops. It is
very true he leaves a surf, a sort of kelp and drift-
wood, and trash, the scum, the idlers, and the
cowards and prostitutes of his tribe, as the sea leaves
weeds and drift and kelp. But the true Indian is to
be found only in his fastnesses or on the heights,
gun in hand.

CHAPTER X.

GIVE US THIS DAY OUR DAILY BREAD.

THE boy had not moved. I believe he had not lifted his eyes. The sharp wind, pitching up and down and across, cut him no doubt, on the one hand, while the burning wigwams scorched him on the other; but he did not move.

The Prince had stood there all this time like a king, turning sometimes to watch this man or that, but never going aside, never giving way an inch for any one. They went around him, they avoided him, or deferred to him in every way possible. From the very moment he came down from the bluff to the bank of the river, and they saw him in their midst, they felt the presence of a master and a man.

I had always said to myself, "This man is of royal blood. This man was born to lead and control." To me he had always stood, like Saul, a head and shoulders above his fellows. I had always believed him a king of men, and now I knew it.

He took the little girl by the hand, folded her robe about her gently as if she had been a Chris-

THE PRINCE SMILED, STOOPED, AND PICKED UP HIS CLUB, AND PUT IT IN HIS HAND.

tian born, looked to her moccasins, and then cast
about to see who should take and provide for the
boy.   The last man was going — gone!

There was a look of pain and trouble in the face
of the Prince.   There was not a crust of bread in
the cabin; a poor place to which to take the two
starved children, to be sure.

The cast of care blew on with the wind; then
with the same old look of confidence and self-pos-
session he went up to the Indian boy, took him
by the thin little arm, and bade him arise and
follow.

The boy started.   He did not understand, and
then he understood perfectly.   He stood up taller
than before.   His face looked fierce and bitter,
and his hands lifted as if he would strike.   The
Prince smiled, stooped and picked up his club, and
put it in his hand.   This conquered him.   He
stood it against the stone on which he had sat, took
up a robe that lay under his feet, fastened his moccasin strings, and we moved away together and in
silence.

The little girl would look up now and then, and
endeavor to be pleasant and do cunning things;
but this boy with his club tucked under his robe
did not look up, nor down, nor around him.

There were some dead that lay in the way; he
did not notice them. He walked across them as if
they had been clay. What could he have been
thinking of ?

I know very well what I do; how unpopular and
unprofitable it is to speak a word for this weak and
unfriended people. Fate seems to have the matter
in hand, for in the last decade they have lost more
ground than in the fifty preceding years. Cannon
are mounted on their strongholds, even on the
summits of the Rocky Mountains. Bayonets
bristle in their forests of the north, and sabers flash
along the plains of the Apache. There is no one
to speak for them now, not one. If there was I
should be silent.

Game and fish have their seasons to come and go,
as regular as the flowers. Now the game go to the
hills, now to the valleys, to winter, now to the
mountains, to bring forth their young. You break
in upon their habits by pushing settlements here
and there. With the fish you do the same by building dams and driving steamboats, and you break
the whole machinery and stop their increase. Then
the Indians must starve, or push over onto the
hunting and fishing grounds of another tribe. This
makes war. The result is they fight — fight like

dogs! almost like Christians! Here is the whole trouble in a nut-shell.

Let us, sometimes, look down into this thing honestly, try and find the truth, and understand.

Even the ocean has a bottom.

We reached the cabin, and built a roaring fire.

" Stand your club there in the corner, Klamat," said the Prince to the boy, " and come to the fire. This is your home now." The boy understood the signs and the softened speech, and did as he was bid, not as a slave, but proud and unbending as a chief in council.

The little girl had washed her hands and face, thrown back her long, luxuriant hair, and stood drying herself by the fire, quite at home.

Two more mouths to feed, and where was the bread to come from?

Soon the Prince went out and left us there. He returned in a little while with a loaf of bread.

Where did he get it? I never knew.

He divided it with a knife carefully into three pieces, gave first to the Indian boy, then to the Indian girl, and then to me. Then he stood there a moment, looked a little embarrassed, but finally said something about wood and went out.

We ate our bread as the ax smote and echoed against the pine-log outside.

A certain strong magnet attracts, from out the grains of gold, all the ironstone and black sand to itself. It seemed there was something in the nature of this man that attracted all the helpless, and weak, and worthless to his side. He had not sought these little savages. That would have been folly, if not an absolute wrong to them. There was, perhaps, not another man in camp as little capable of caring for them as he.

To see those Indians eat — daintily, only a little bit at a time, then put it under the robe, stealthily, and look about them; then a memory, and the head would bend and the eyes go down; then the little piece of bread would be withdrawn, eyed wistfully, a morsel broken off, and then the piece again returned beneath the robe, to be again withdrawn, as they found it impossible to resist the hunger that consumed them.

But Indians are strangely preservative, and these had just endured a bitter school. They had learned the importance of hoarding a bit for to-morrow, and even the next morning had quite a piece of bread still. How could they suppose that any one would provide, or attempt to provide, for them the next day?

The Prince came in at last from the dusk, and we all went out and helped to bring the wood from the snow.

I am bound to say that I suddenly grew vastly in my own estimation that evening. Up to this time I had been the youngest person in all the camp, the most helpless, the least of all. Here was a change. Here were persons more helpless than myself; some one now that I could advise, direct, dictate to, and patronize.

There must be a point in each man's life when he becomes a man — turns from the ways of a boy.

I daresay any man can date his manhood from some event, from some little circumstance that seemed to invest him with a sort of majesty, and dignify him, in his own estimation, at least, with manhood. A man must first be his own disciple. If he does not first believe himself a man, he may be very sure the world will not believe it.

We sat late by the fire that night. The little girl leaned against the wall by the fireside and slept, but the boy seemed only to brighten and awake as the night went on. He looked into the fire. What did he see? What were his thoughts?

What faces were there? Fire, and smoke, and blood — the dead!

Down before the fire in their fur robes we laid the little Indians to sleep, and sought our blankets in the bunks against the wall.

Through the night one arose, and then the other, and stirred the fire silently and lay down. Indians never let their fires go out in their lodges in time of peace. It is thought a bad omen, and then it is inconvenient, and certainly not the thing to do in the winter.

The Prince was up early the next morning. He could not sleep. Why? Starve yourself a week, and you will understand. I did not think or ask myself then why he could not sleep. I know now.

He went to town at daybreak. Then, when we had rolled a back-log into the spacious fire-place, and built a fire under my direction, a new style of architecture to the Indians, with a fore-stick on the stone and irons, and a heap of kindling-wood in the center, I induced Klamat to wash his face, and helped him to wash the blood from his hair in a pan of tepid water.

The little girl, without any direction, made her toilet, poor child, in a simple, natural way, with a careful regard for the effect of falls of dark hair on her brown shoulders and about her face; and then we all sat down and looked at the fire, and at each other in silence.

Soon the Prince returned, and, wonderful to tell, he had on his shoulder a sack of flour.

His face was beaming with delight. He took the sack from his shoulder gently, set it on the empty flour-bench in the corner, as carefully and tenderly as if it had been a babe—as if it had been his own firstborn.

The "Doctor" came with him. Not on a professional visit, however, but as a friend, and to see the Indians.

Now, this Doctor was a character, a special part of The Forks. Not a lovely part or an excellent part, in the estimation of either saloon-men or miners, but he filled a place there that had been left blank had he gone away, and that was not altogether because he was the only doctor in the place, but because he was a man of marked individuality.

A man who did not care three straws for the good or ill will of man, and, as a consequence, as is always the fortune of such men when they first appear in a place, was not popular.

He was a small man, a sort of an invalid, and a

man who had no associates whatever. He was
always alone, and never spoke to you if he could
help it.

How the Prince made this man's acquaintance I
do not know. Most likely he had gone to him
that morning deliberately, told him the situation
of things, asked for help, and had it for the asking.
For my part, I had rather have seen almost any
one else enter the cabin. I did not like him from
the first time that I ever saw him.

" Come here, Paquita," said the Doctor, as he
sat down on the three-legged stool by the fire, and
held out his hand to the Indian girl. She drew
her robe modestly about her bosom, and went up
to the man, timid but pleasantly.

I knew no more of this Doctor, or his name,
than of the other men around me.

He had come into the camp as a doctor, had pill-
bags and a book or two, and was called the Doctor.

Had another doctor come, he would have been
called Doctor Brown, or Smith, or Jones, provided
that neither of these names, or the name given him
by the camp, was the name given him by his
parents. I know a doctor who wore the first
beaver hat into a camp and was called Doctor Tile.
He could not get rid of that name. If he had died

in the camp, Doctor Tile would have been the name written on the pine board at his head.

"I will bake some bread, Doctor, for my babies;" and the Prince threw off his coat and rolled up his sleeves, and went to work. He opened the mouth of his burden on the bunk, thrust in his hand, drew out the yellow flour in the gold-pan, sprinkled in some salt, poured in cold water from the bucket, and soon had a luscious cake baking before the fire in the frying-pan.

Little Klamat meantime had retreated to his club, and stood with his back to the corner, with his head down, but at the same time watching the Doctor from under his hair, as a cat watches a mouse; only he was not the cat in this case, by a great deal.

The Doctor talked but little, and then only in an enigmatical sort of a way, with the Prince. He did· not notice me, and that contributed to my instinctive dislike. Soon he took leave, and we four ate bread together.

A wind came up the Klamat from the sea that night, soft and warm enough to drip the icicles from the cabin eaves, and make the drooping trees along the river bank raise their heads from the snow as if with hope.

The Doctor came frequently and spent the evening as the weeks went by. The butchers' mules came braying down the trail erelong, and we needed bread and meat no more. ·

The thunder boomed away to the west one night as if it had been the trump of resurrection ; a rain set in, and the next morning Humbug Creek, as if it had heard a Gabriel blow, had risen and was rushing toward the Klamat and calling to the sea.·

Some birds flew out, squirrels left the rocks and kept running up and down the pines, and places where the snow had melted off and left brown burs and quills and little shells. The backbone of the winter storm was broken.

CHAPTER XI.

SUNSHINE.

THE sunshine follows the rain. There was a sort of general joyousness. The Prince was now a king, it seemed to me. He had fought a battle with fate against him; fought it silent, patient, and alone; he had conquered, and was glad.

The great hero is born of the long, long struggle. Who cannot go down to battle with banners, with trumps and the tramp of horses? Who cannot fight for a day in a line of a thousand strong, with the eyes of the world upon him? But the man who fights a battle coolly, quietly, patiently and alone, with no one to applaud or approve, as the strife goes on through all the weary year, and after all to have no reward but that of his own conscience, the calm delight of a duty well performed, is God's own hero.

He is knighted and ennobled there, when the fight is won, and he wears thenceforth the spurs of gold and an armor of invulnerable steel.

We went down again among the boulders in the bed of the creek. The Prince swung his pick, I

8   (113)

shoveled the thrown-out earth, and the little Indians would come and look on and wonder, and lend a hand in an awkward sort of a way for a few minutes at a time, then go back to the cabin or high up on the hills in the sun, following whatever pursuit they chose.

The Prince did not take it upon himself to direct or dictate what they should do, but watched their natural inclinations and actions with the keenest interest.

He loved freedom too well himself to attempt to fetter these little unfortunates with rules and forms that he himself did not hold in too great respect; and, as for taxing them to labor, they were yet weak, and but poorly recovered from the effects of the famine on the Klamat.

Besides, he had no disposition to reduce them to the Christian slavery that was then being introduced, and still obtains, up about Mount Shasta, wherever any of the Indians survive.

The girl developed an amiable and gentle nature, but the boy showed anything but that from the first. He always went out of the cabin whenever strangers entered, would often spend days alone, out of sight of every one, and stubbornly refused to speak a word of English. At the end of weeks he was untamed

as ever, and evidently untamable. The Prince
had procured him a cheap suit of clothes, something after the fashion of the miner's dress; but he
despised it, and would only wear his shirt with the
right arm free and naked, the red sleeve tucked in
or swinging about his body. He submitted to
have his hair trimmed, but refused to wear a hat.

The first great epoch of his civilized life was the
receipt of a knife as a gift from the Prince. It was
more to him than diamonds to a bride. He kept
it with him everywhere; slept with it always. It
was to him as a host of companions.

Sometimes he talked in the Indian tongue to the
girl, but only when he thought no one noticed or
heard him.

The girl was quite the other way. She took to
domestic matters eagerly, learned to talk in a few
weeks, after a fashion, and was most anxious to be
useful. She had a singular talent for drawing.
One day she made an excellent charcoal picture of
Mount Shasta, on the cabin door, and was delighted
when she saw the Prince take pride in her work.
She was eager to do everything, and insisted on
doing all the cooking.

She had a great idea of the use of salt, and often
an erroneous one. For instance, one morning she

put salt in the coffee as well as in the beef and
beans. I think it was an experiment of hers —
that she was so anxious to please and make things
palatable, she put it in to improve the taste. I
can very well understand how she thought it all
over, and said to herself, " Now, if a little pinch of
this white substance adds to the beans, why will
it not contribute to the flavor of the coffee? " Once
she put sugar on the meat instead of salt, but the
same mistake never happened twice.

I must admit that she was deceitful, somewhat;
not willfully, but innocently so. In fact, had anything of importance been involved, she would have
stood up and told the whole simple truth with a
perfect indifference to results. She did this once,
I know, when she had done an improper thing, in
a way that made us trust and respect her. But
she did so much like to seem wise about things of
which she was wholly ignorant. When she had
learned to talk she one day pretended to Klamat
to also be able to read and understand what was
written on the bills of the butchers. Her ambition
seemed to be to appear learned in that she knew
the least about. But all that is so much like many
people you meet, that I know you are prepared to
call her half-civilized, even in these few weeks.

This sort of innocent deceit is no new thing, particularly in women. And I rather like it. Go on
to one of the fashionable streets to-day in America, and there you will find that the lady who has
the least amount of natural hair has invariably the
largest amount of artificial fix-ups on her head.
This rule is almost infallible; it has hardly the traditional exception to testify to its truth.

And I am not sure but that nature herself is a
little deceitful. The dead and leafless oaks have
the richest growth of ivy, as if to make the world
believe that the trees are thriving like the bay. All
about the mouths of caves, all openings in the
earth, old wells and pits, the rankest growths
abound, as if to say, here is no wound in the breast
of earth! here is even the richest and the choicest
spot upon her surface.

To go further into a new field. If a true woman
loves you truly, she fortifies against it in every possible way as a weak place in her nature. She
tries to deceive, not only the world, but herself.
To keep out the eyes of the inquisitive, she would
build a barricade to the moon. She would not be
seen to whisper with you for the world. Yet, if she
loved you less, she would laugh and talk and whisper

by the hour, and think nothing of it.   I like such
deceit as that.   It is natural.

The miners were at work like beavers.   Up the
stream and down the stream the pick and shovel
clanged against the rock and gravel from dawn until darkness came down out of the forests above
them and took possession of the place.

The Prince worked on patiently, industriously
with the rest, with reasonable success and first-rate
promise of fortune.   The pent-up energies of the
camp were turned loose, and the stream ran thick
and yellow with sediment from pans, rockers, toms,
sluices and flumes.

Spring came sudden and full grown from the
south.   She blew up in a fleet of sultry clouds from
the Mexican seas, along the Californian coast.

At first she hardly set foot in the cañon.   The
sun came down to us only about noontide, and
then only tarried long enough to shoot a few bright
shafts through the dusk and dense pine-tops at the
banks of snow beneath, and spring did not like the
place as well as the open, sunny plains over by the
city, and toward the Klamat lakes.   But at last she
came to take possession.   She planted her banners
on places the sun made bare, and put up signs and
landmarks not to be misunderstood.

The balm and alder burst in leaf, and catkins drooped and dropped from willows in the water, till you had thought a legion of woolly caterpillars were drifting to the sea. Still the place was not to be surrendered without a struggle. It was one of winter's strongholds. He had been driven, day after day, in a march of many a thousand miles. He had retreated from Mexico to within sight of Mount Shasta, and here he turned on his pursuer. One night he came boldly down and laid hands on the muddy little stream, and stretched a border of ice all up and down its edges; spread frost-work, white and beautiful, on pick, and tom, and sluice, and flume and cradle, and made the miners curse him to his beard. He cut down the banners of the spring that night, lamb-tongue, Indian turnip and catella, and took possession as completely as of old.

But, when the sun came up at last, he let go his hold upon the stream, took off his stamp from pick and pan, and tom, and sluice and cradle, and crept in silence into the shade of trees and up the mountain side against the snow.

And now the spring came back with a double force and strength. She planted California lilies, fair and bright as stars, tall as little flag-staffs, along the mountain side, and up against the winter's barricade of snow, and proclaimed possession absolute through her messengers, the birds, and we were very glad.

Paquita gathered blossoms in the sun, threw her long hair back, and bounded like a fawn along the hills. Klamat took his club and knife, drew his robe only the closer about him in the sun, and went out gloomy and somber in the mountains. Sometimes he would be gone all night.

At last the baffled winter abandoned even the wall that lay between us and the outer world, and drew off all his forces to Mount Shasta. He retreated above the timber line, but he retreated not an inch beyond. There he sat down with all his strength. He planted his white and snowy tent upon this everlasting fortress, and laughed at the world below him.

CHAPTER XII.

"A MAN FOR BREAKFAST."

"Now, that we have got an alcalde," said a man one day, "why not put him to work?"

There had been a pretty general feeling against those who took part in the murder of the Indians by the miners, and this man who was always boiling over on some subject, and was brimful of energy, went and laid the case before the alcalde and instituted a prosecution. Here was a sensation! The court sent a constable to arrest a prisoner with a verbal warrant, and the man came into "court," followed by half the town, gave verbal bonds for his appearance next Sunday, and the court adjourned to that day.

Sides were taken at once. The idlers, of course, all taking sides with the prisoner; the miners mostly going the other way. The assassins were active in getting evidence out of the way, making friends with the alcalde, and intimidating all who dared express sympathy with the Indians.

The Indian boy came home that night, beaming with delight. His black eyes flashed like the eyes of a cat in the dark. He had always seemed so passive and sullen, that we had come to believe he had no life or passion in him.

He talked to Paquita eagerly, and made all kinds of gestures; put his fingers about his neck, stabbed himself with an imaginary knife, threw himself toward the fire, and shot, with an imaginary gun at an imaginary prisoner. Would he be hung, stabbed, burnt or shot? The boy was so eager and excited that once or twice he broke out into pretty fair English at some length, the first he had ever been heard to utter.

The Doctor was unpopular. In fact, doctors usually are in the mines. Whether this is because nine-tenths of those who are there are impostors, or whether it is because miners give open expression to a natural dislike that strong men feel for the man to whose ministry we all have to submit ourselves some day, I do not pretend to say.

Even the Indian boy disliked the Doctor bitterly, and one day flew at him, without any cause, and clutched a handful of hair from his half-bald head. The alcalde, too, disliked the Doctor, and only the evening before the trial some one, passing the cabin, heard the alcalde call the Doctor a fool to his teeth. ,

That was a feather in the alcalde's hat, in the eyes of The Forks, but a bad sign for the Doctor. The Doctor should have knocked him down, said The Forks.

The day of the trial came, and the big prosecutor, in respect for the court and the occasion, buttoned up his flannel shirt, hid his hairy bosom, and gave over his gin and peppermint during all the examination.

The prisoner was named "Spades." Whether it was because he looked so like the black, squatty Jack of Spades I do not know; but I should say he was indebted to his likeness to that right or left bower for his name.

There was not the slightest doubt that he had deliberately murdered two or three Indian children, butchered them, as they crouched on the ground; but there were grave doubts as to what the alcalde would do in the case, for he had been pretty plainly told that he must not hold the man to answer.

A low, wretched man was this—the lowest in the camp; but he stood between others of a more respectable character and danger. His fortune in the matter was a prophecy of theirs. The prisoner was nearly drunk as he took his seat. He sat with

his hat on. In fact, miners, in the matter of wear-
ing hats, would make first-class Israelites.

" Ef I ain't out o' this by dark," said Spades, as
he jerked his head over his shoulder and spirted ·
a stream of amber at the back-log, " I'll sun somebody's moccasins, see if I don't." And he looked
straight at the alcalde, who settled down uneasily
in his seat, and placed his new beaver hat on the
table between himself and the prisoner as a sort of
barricade.

Two or three gamblers, good enough men in
their way, acted as attorneys for Spades. The big
prosecutor proved by his witnesses how Spades
had butchered the babes down on the Klamat, in
detail.

The other side did not ask any questions. The
attorneys whispered a moment among themselves,
and then one of them got up, took the stand, and
gravely asserted that on that day, and at the very
moment described, he was playing poker with
Spades at two bits a corner. Then another arose
with the same account ; and then another. It was
the clearest *alibi* possible.

This was the first attempt to introduce law prac-
tice at The Forks, and no wonder that it did not
work well, and that some things were forgotten.

All were new hands — court, counsel, and nearly all present, here witnessed their first trial.

They all had forgotten to have their witnesses sworn.

The testimony being all in, the "Court" proceeded solemnly to sum up the case. In conclusion, it said, "You will observe that, as a rule, the further we go from the surface of things the nearer we get to the bottom." This brought cheers and wavings of hats, and the Court repeated, "I am free to say that the Court has gone diligently into the depths of this case, and that, as a rule, the further you get from the surface of things the nearer you get to the bottom. The case looked dark indeed against the prisoner at first; but the Court has gone to the bottom of the matter and he is now white as snow."

"Hear! hear! hear!" shouted a man from Sydney, who always hobbled a little as if he dragged a chain when he walked.

"Snow is good!" said a miner between his teeth, as he looked at the black visage of the prisoner.

"You see," continued the alcalde, "that things are often not so black as they first appear, particularly if they are only fairly washed."

" Particularly if they are white-washed ! " said the big prosecutor, as he turned to the bar, swallowed his gin and peppermint, and left the saloon in disgust.

All this time a tawny little figure had stood back in the corner unseen, perhaps, by any one. It was Klamat with his club. He had watched with the eyes of a hawk the whole proceeding. He had drank in every sentence, and had never once taken his eyes from the Court or the prisoner.

When the alcalde decreed the prisoner free, and the Court adjourned, and all ranged themselves in a long, single file before the bar, calling out " Cocktail," " Tom-and-Jerry," " Brandy-smash," " Ginsling," " Lightning straight," " Forty-rod," and so on, he slipped out.

The Doctor quarreled with the alcalde.

" That little doctor 'll put a bug in his soup for him yet, see 'f he don't," said some one that evening at the saloon.

" All right, let him," said a man, who stood at the bar, in gum-boots and with a gold-pan under his left arm. " All right, let him," said the bearded sovereign, as he threw back his head and opened his mouth. " It's not my circus, nor won't be my funeral;" and he wiped his beard and went out saying to himself:

> "Fight dog, and fight bar,
> Thar's no dog of mine thar."

The Prince, with that clear common-sense which always came to the surface, had foreseen the whole affair so far as the trial was concerned, and had remained at home hard at work.

The next morning the butcher shouted down from the cabin, as he weighed out the steaks : " A man for breakfast up in town, I say! a man for breakfast up in town, and I'll bet you can't guess who it is."

" Who? "

" The alcalde! "

The man had been stabbed to death not far from his own door, some time in the night, perhaps just before retiring. There were three distinct mortal wounds in the breast. There had evidently been a short, hard struggle for life, for in one hand he clutched a lock of somebody's hair. That long, soft, silken, half curling, yellow German hair of the Doctor's, that grew on the sides of his head — there was not to be found another lock of hair like this in the mountains.

The dead man had not been robbed. That was

a point in the Doctor's favor.   He had been met in
the front, had not been poisoned, or stabbed or
shot in the back ; that was another very strong
point in the Doctor's favor.

*   *   *   *   *   *   *

As a rule, a funeral in the mines is a mournful
thing.   It is the saddest and most pitiful spectacle
I have ever seen.   The contrast of strength and
weakness is brought out here in such a way that
you must turn aside or weep when you behold it.
To see those strong, rough men, long-haired,
bearded and brown, rugged and homely-looking,
with something of the grizzly in their great, awkward movements, now take up one of their number,
straightened in the rough pine box, in his miner's
dress, and carry him up, up on the hill in silence —
it is sad beyond expression.

He has come a long way, he has journeyed by
land or sea for a year, he has toiled and endured,
and denied himself all things for some dear object
at home, and now, after all, he must lie down in the
forests of the Sierras, and turn on his side and die.
No one to kiss him, no one to bless him, and say
" good-bye," only as a woman can, and close the
weary eyes, and fold the hands in their final rest:
and then, at the grave, how awkward — how silent!

How'they would like to look at each other and say
something, yet, how they hold down their heads, or
look away to the horizon, lest they should meet
each other's eyes. Lest some strong man should
see the tears that went silently down from the eyes
of another over his beard and onto the leaves

* * * * * * *

The Doctor had appeared out of place in this
camp from the first. Every one seemed to feel
that—perhaps no one felt it more keenly than himself.

There are people, it seems to me, who go all
through life looking for the place where they be-
long and never finding it. This to me is a very
sad sight. They seem to fit in no place on top of
the earth.

I had always hated and feared the man till now.
But the feeling against him now aroused a sort of
antagonism in my nature, that always has, and I
expect always will, come to the surface on such
occasions on the side of the despised, perfectly re-
gardless of propriety, self-interest, or any consideration whatever.

If a man has succeeded and is glad, let him go
his way. What should I have to do with him?

And maybe, often, there is a kind of subtle wis-

dom in this view of men.` I think it is born ·of the
fact that your ostentatious, prosperous man, your
showy rich man of America, is so very, very poor,
that you do not care to call him your neighbor.
It is true he has horses and houses and land and
gold, but these horses and houses and lands and
coins, are all in the world he has. When he dies
these will all remain and the world will lose nothing
whatever. His death will not make even a ripple
in the tide of life. His family, whom he has taught
to worship gold, will forget him in their new estates.
In their hearts they will be glad that he has gone.
They will barter and haggle with the stone-cutter
toiling for his bread, and for a starve-to-death price
they will lift a marble shaft above his head with an
iron fence around it—typical, cold, and soulless!

Poor man, since he took nothing away that one
could miss, what a beggar he must have been. The
poor and unhappy never heard of him: the world
has not lost a thought. Not a note missed, not a
word was lost in the grand, sweet song of the universe when he died.

It was remarkable how suddenly the Indian children sprung up with the summer. No one could
have recognized in this neat, modest, sensitive girl,
and this silent, savage-looking boy, who sometimes

PAQUITA.

looked almost a man, the two starved, naked little creatures of half a year before.

There was a little lake belted by wild red roses and salmon berries, and fretted by overhanging ferns under the great firs that shut out the sun save in little spars and bars of light that fell through upon a bench of the hills; a sort of lily pond, only half a pistol-shot across, at the bottom of a waterfall, and clear as sunshine itself. Here Paquita would go often and alone to pass her idle hours. I chanced to see her there on the rim, walking against the sun, and looking into the water as she moved forward, now and then back, across her shoulder, as a maiden in a glass preparing for a ball. She had just been made glad with her first new dress — red, and decorated with ribbons, made gay, and of many colors. The poor child was studying herself in the waters.

This was not vanity; no doubt there was a deal of satisfaction, a sort of quiet pride, in this, but it was something higher, also. A desire to study grace, to criticise her movements in this strange, and to her, lovely dress, and learn to move with the most perfect propriety. She practiced this often. The finger lifted sometimes, the head bowed, then the hands in rest, and the head thrown back, she would walk back and forth for hours, contemplating herself, and catching the most graceful motion from the water.

What a rich, full, and generous mouth was hers —frank as the noonday. Beware of people with small mouths, they are not generous. A full, rich mouth, impulsive and passionate, is the kind of mouth to trust, to believe in, to ask a favor of, and to give kind words to.

There are as many kinds of mouths as there are crimes in the catalogue of sins. There is the mouth for hash! —thick-lipped, coarse, and expressionless, a picket of teeth behind. Bah! Then there is the thin-lipped, sour-apple mouth, sandwiched in between a sharp chin and thin nose. Look out!

There are mischievous mouths, ruddy and full of fun, that you would like to be on good terms with if you had time; and then there is the rich, full mouth, with dimples dallying and playing about it like ripples in a shade, half sad, half glad—a mouth to love. Such was Paquita's. A rose, but not yet opened; only a bud that in another summer would unfold itself wide to the sun.

CHAPTER XIII.

BONE AND SINEW.

How we wrought! the Prince and I, patiently and industriously. So did thousands above us and below us; there was a clang of picks and shovels, the smiting of steel on the granite, a sound through the sable forests, an echoing up the far hill-sides like the march of an army to battle, clashing the sword and buckler.

Every man that wrought there, worked for an object. There was a payment to be met at home; a mortgage to be lifted. The ambition of one I knew was to buy a little home for his parents; another had orphan sisters to provide for; this had an invalid mother. This had a bride, and that one the promise of a bride. Every miner there had a history, a plan, a purpose.

Every miner there who bent above the boulders, and toiled on silently under the dark-plumed pines and the shadows of the steep and stupendous mountains, was a giant in body and soul.

Never since the days of Cortez, has there been gathered together such a hardy and brave body of

men as these first men of the Pacific.   When it took
six months' voyaging round the Horn, and immi-
nent perils, with like dangers and delays, to cross
the isthmus or the continent, then the weak of heart
did not attempt it, and the weak of body died on
the way.   The result was a race of men worthy of
the land.

There was another segregation and sifting out
after the Pacific was reached.   There lay the mines
open to all who would work; no capital but a pick
and pan required.   The most manly and independ-
ent life on earth.   At night you had your pay in
your hand, your reward weighed out in virgin gold.
If you made five, ten, fifty, or a thousand dollars
that day, you made it from the fall of no man; no
decline of stocks or turn in trade which carried
some man to the bottom, brought you to the top;
no speculation, no office, no favor, only your own
two hands and your strong, true heart, without
favor from any man.   You had contributed that
much to the commerce of the world.   If there is
any good in gold, you had done that much good to
the world, besides the good to yourself.

*   *   *   *   *   *   *

The Doctor in the meantime ranged around the
hill-sides, wrote some, gathered some plants, and

seemed altogether the most listless, wretched, miserable man you could conceive. He made his home in our cabin now, and rarely went to town ; for when he did so, some one of the hangers-on about the saloons was sure to insult him. Sometimes, however, he would be obliged to go, such as when some accident or severe illness would compel the miners to send for him, and he never refused to attend. On one of these occasions, Spades, half drunk and wholly vicious, caught the Doctor by the throat as he met him in the trail near town, and shook him.

Spades boasted he had made his old teeth rattle like rocks in a rocker. The Doctor said nothing, but got off as best he could and came home. He did not even mention the matter to any one.

Shortly after this Spades was found dead. He was found just as the alcalde had been found, close to his cabin door, with mortal stabs in the breast.

There was talk of a mob. This thing of killing people in the night, even though they were the most worthless men of the camp, and even though they were killed in a way that suggested something like fair play, and revenge rather than robbery, was not to be indulged in with impunity. Some of the idlers got together to pass resolutions, and take

some steps in the matter, as Spades lay stretched
out under an old blue soldier-coat on a pine slab
that had many dark stains across and along its
rugged surface, but they fell into an exciting game
of poker, at ten dollars a corner, and the matter
for the time was left to rest. No Antony came to
hold up the dead Cæsar's mantle, and poor Spades
was buried much as they had buried the alcalde a
short time before.

Some one consulted the Giant on the subject,
about the time of the funeral, as he stood at the
bar of the Howlin' Wilderness for his gin and peppermint. The Giant was something of a mouth-
piece for the miners, not that he was a recognized
leader ; miners, as a rule, decline to be led, but
rather that he knew what they thought on most
subjects, and preferred to act with them and express their thoughts, rather than incline to the
idlers about The Forks. He drank his gin in
silence, set down his glass, and said in an oracular
sort of way, as if to himself, when passing out of
the door :

" Well, let 'em rip ; it's dog eat dog, anyhow !"

But it was evident that this matter would not
blow over easily. True, there was no magistrate

in camp yet, but there was a live sheriff over in the city and the sheriff wanted work.

The Doctor went on as usual, avoiding men a little more than before.

CHAPTER XIV.

A STORM IN THE SIERRAS.

VIRGIN gold, like truth, lies at the bottom. It is a great task in the placer mines, as a rule, particularly in the streams, to get on the bed-rock to open a claim and strike a lead. When this is done the rest is simple enough. You have only to keep your claim open, to see that the drain is not clogged, the tail race kept open, and that the water does not break in and fill up your excavation, by which you have reached the bed-rock. All this the Prince and I had accomplished. The summer was sufficiently cool to be tolerable in toil : the season was unusually healthy, and all was well.

At night, when the flush of the sun would be blown from the tree tops to the clouds, we two would sit at the cabin door in the gloaming, and look across and up, far up, into the steep and sable skirting forest of firs, and listen to the calls of the cat-bird, or the coyote lifting his voice in a plaintive monologue for his mate on the other side.

Paquita, who at such times sat not far off, had a

great deal to tell about Mount Shasta. She had been on the side beyond. In fact, her home was there, she said, and she described the whole land in detail. A country sloping off gradually toward the east and south ; densely timbered, save little dimples of green prairies, alive with game, dotted down here and there, buried in the dark and splendid forests on the little trout streams that wound still and crooked through wood and meadow.

She had been out here on the Klamat on a visit, with her mother and others, the fall and winter before. She said they had come down from the lakes in canoes. She also insisted strongly that her father was a great chief of the Modocs and mountain Shastas.

Indians are great travelers, far greater than is generally believed, and it was quite reasonable to take that part of the young lady's story as literally true ; but the part about her father being a great chief was set down as one of her innocent fictions by which she wished to dignify herself, and appear of some importance in the eyes of the Prince.

Still as there had been quite a sensation in camp about new mines in that direction, it was interesting to talk to one who had been through the country, and could give us some accurate account of it. After

that, finding the Prince was interested enough to
listen, she would take great pleasure in describing
the country, character and habits of the Indians, and
the kind of game with which the forest abounded.

She would map out on the ground with a stick
the whole country, as you would draw a chart on
the black-board.

The feeling against the Doctor had not yet blown
over. It was pretty generally understood that the
sheriff or a deputy from across the mountain would
soon be over with a warrant for his apprehension.

Why not escape? There are some popular errors
of opinion that are amusing. Men suppose that if
a man is in the mountains he is safe, hid away, and
secure; that he has only to step aside in the brush
and be seen no more.

As a rule, it is safer to be in the heart of a city.
Here was a camp of a few thousand men. Each
man knew the face of his neighbor. There was
but one way to enter this camp, but one way to go
out; that way led to the city. We were in a sac,
the further end of a cave, as it were. You could
not go this way, or that, through the mountains
alone. There were no trails; there was no food.
You would get lost; you would starve.

Here, in that day, at least, if a man did wrong

he could not hide.   The finger of God pointed him out to all.

Late one September day it grew intensely sultry; there was a haze in the sky and a circle about the sun.   There was not a breath.   The perspiration came out and stood on the brow, even as we rested in the shadow of the pines.   A singular haze; such a day, it is said, as precedes earthquakes.

The black crickets ceased to sing; the striped lizards slid quick as ripples across the rocks, and birds went swift as arrows overhead, but uttered no cry.   There was not a sound in the air nor on the earth.

Paquita came rushing down to the claim, pale and excited.   She lifted her two hands above her head as she stood on the bank, and called to us to come up from the mine.   " Come," she cried, " there will be a storm.   The trees will blow and break against each other.   There will be a flood, a sea, a river in the mountains.   Come!"   She swayed her body to and fro, and the trees began to sway above her on the hills, but not a breath had touched the mines.

Then it grew almost dark; we fairly had to feel our way up the ladder.

There was a roar like the sea — loud, louder. Nearer now the trees began to bend and turn and interweave and smite and crush and lurch until their tops were like one black and boiling sea.

Fast, faster, the rain in great warm drops began to strike us in the face, as we hastened up the hill to the shelter of the cabin. At the door we turned to look. The darkness of death was upon us; we could hear the groans and the battling of the trees, the howling of the tempest, but all was darkness, blackness, save when the lightning cleft the heavens.

A sheet of flame — as if the hand of God had thrust out through the dark and smote the mountain side with a sword of fire.

And then the thunder shook the earth till it trembled, as if Shasta had been shaken loose and broken from its foundation. No one spoke. The lightning lit the cabin like a bonfire. Klamat stood there in the cabin by his club and gun. There was in his face a grim delight. The Doctor lay on his face in his bunk, hiding his eyes in his two hands.

No one undressed that night in the camp.

The next morning the fury of the storm was over. We ventured out and looked down into the stream. It was nearly large enough to float a steamer. The

claim was filled up as level as when we first took it
from the hands of the Creator.   Ten feet of water
flowed swift and muddy over it toward the Klamat
and the sea.

Logs, boards, shingles, rockers, toms, sluices,
flumes, pans, riffles, aprons, went drifting, bobbing,
dodging down the angry river like a thousand
eager swimmers.

The storm had stolen everything, and was rushing with his plunder straight as could be to the sea,
as if he feared that dawn should catch him in the
camp, and the miners come upon him to reclaim
their goods.

Every miner in the camp was ruined.   No man
had dreamed of this.   Maybe a few had saved up
a little fortune, but, as a rule, all their fortunes lay
in the folds of the next few months.

Brave men! they said nothing; they set their
teeth, looked things squarely in the face, but did
not complain.   One man, however, who watched
the flood from a point on the other side and saw his
flume swept away, swung his old slouched hat,
danced a sort of savage hokee-pokee, and sang:

> "O, everything is lovely,
> And the goose hangs high!"

We two had not saved much money.   And what

portion of that had I earned? I could not well
claim a great deal, surely. How much would be
left when the debts were paid—the butcher and
the others ? True, the claim was valuable, but it
had no value now — not so much as a sack of
flour. There were too many wanting to get away,
and men had not yet learned the worth of a
mine. Sometimes in these days new excitements
would tap a camp, drain it dry, and not leave a soul
to keep the coyotes from taking possession of the
cabins.

"What will you do? "said the Prince to me, as we
sat on the bank. "We cannot reach the bed-
rock again till far into the next year. What will
you do?"

" May I stay with you? "

The strong man reached me his two hands —" As
long as I live and you live, my little one, and
there is a blanket to my name, we will sleep under
it together. But we will leave this camp. I
have hated it from the first. I have grown old here
in a year. I cannot breathe in this narrow
cañon, with its great walls against the clouds. We
will go."

CHAPTER XV.

A HOUSE TO LET.

THAT night the Prince talked a long time with Paquita about the new country on the other side of Shasta, and, putting her account and my brief knowledge of the country together, he resolved to go there, where gold, according to her story, was to be had almost for the picking up, if the Indians did not interfere.

The next morning this man rested his elbows on the table, and, with his face buried in his hands, was a long time silent.

" Pack up," he said, at last, to the little girl.

In a few moments she stood by his side, with a red calico dress and some ribbons tied up in a handkerchief in one hand, and a pair of moccasins in the other.

The Doctor was anxious to get away — more anxious, perhaps, than any one. For what had the camp been to him? If I could have had my way or say, I would have left this mysterious, sad-faced, silent man behind.

I think the Prince would have done the same.

We cannot always have our own way, even with ourselves.

Why does the man not do thus and so, we say? What is there to hinder him? Who shall say yea or nay? Is he not his own master? No. No man is his own master who has a conscience.

If this man had been of stronger will, had he not been so utterly helpless and friendless, we could have left him, and would have left him gladly; as it was, it was not a matter of choice at all.

Ponies were scarce, and mules were high priced and hard to get, but the Doctor was not so poor as we, and he put his money all in the Prince's hands. So we had a tolerable outfit.

A very little pony would answer for me, the commonest kind could bear Paquita and her extra dress, while Klamat could walk and make his own way through the woods, like a grayhound.

The Prince procured a great double-barreled shot-gun, throwing buckshot by the handful, for himself, and pistols for all, for we were going into the heart of a hostile country.

An officer, it was rumored, was on the watch for the Doctor, and Klamat prepared to lead us by way of a blind trail, up the mountain side, without passing out by way of The Forks.

One of the most interesting studies, as well as one of the rarest, is that of man in a state of nature. Next to that is the state of man removed from, or above the reach of, all human law, utterly away from what is still more potent to control the actions of men, public opinion — the good or ill will of the world.

As far as my observation has gone, I am bound to say that any expression on the subject would be highly laudatory of the native goodness of man. I should say, as a rule, he, in that state, is brave, generous, and just.

But in civilization I find that the truly just and good man is rarely prominent, he is hardly heard of, while some little, sharp-faced commercial meddler, who never spends or bestows a farthing without first balancing it on his finger, and reckoning how much it will bring him by way of honor in return, is often counted the noblest man among us.

With his moccasins bound tight about his feet, and reaching up so as to embrace the legs of his buckskin pantaloons, his right arm freed from the hateful red-shirt sleeve which hung in freedom at his side, some eagle feathers in his hair, and his rifle on his shoulder, Klamat, with a beaming countenance, led the way from the cabin.

The Prince had assigned him the post of honor,
and he was carried away with delight. He seemed
to forget that he was the only one on foot.   No
doubt he would gladly have given up the red shirt
and buckskins, all but his rifle, with pleasure, at
this supreme moment, had they been required to
insure his position as leader.

Alexander gave away to his friends the last of
the spoils after a great battle.   "And what have
you kept for yourself?" said one.   "Hope and
glory," he answered.

Klamat was an infant Alexander.

I followed, then Paquita, the Doctor next.   The
Prince took up a piece of charcoal from the heap
of charcoal outside the cabin, and wrote, in great,
bold letters on the door:

"TO LET."

We crossed the stream at a cabin below, just as
the miners were beginning to stir.

They seemed to know that something unusual was
taking place.   They straightened themselves in the
fresh light and air, washed their hands and hairy
faces in the gold-pans on the low pine stump by the
door, but tried, or seemed to try, not to observe.

Once across the stream, Klamat led steeply up
the hill for a time, then he would chop and cut to

the right and left in a zigzag route until we had reached the rim of a bench in the mountain. Here he stopped and motioned the Prince to approach, after he had looked back intently into the camp and taken sight by some pines that stood before him.

The Prince rode up to the boy and dismounted; when he had done so, the little fellow lifted three fingers, looked excited, and pointed down upon the old cabin. It was more than a mile away, nearly a mile below; but the sun was pitching directly down upon it, and all things stood out clear and large as life.

Three men rode quickly up to the cabin, leaned from their mules and read the inscription. The leader now dismounted, kicked open the door and entered. It does not take long to search a cabin, without a loft, or even a bed, and the man did not remain a great while within.

Without even taking pains to close the door, to keep out coyotes and other things, as miners do, so that cabins may be habitable for some wayfarer, or fortune-hunters who may not have a house of their own, he hastily mounted and led the party down to the next cabin below.

The miners were evidently at breakfast, for the

man leaned from his saddle and shouted two or three times before any one came out.

The door opened, and a very tall, black-bearded, hairy man came forth, and walked up before the man leaning from his mule.

What was said I do not know, but the bare-headed, hairy man pointed with his long arm up the mountain on the other side, exactly the opposite course from the one we had been taken.

Here the officer said something very loud, pushed back his broad-brimmed hat, and pointed down the stream. The long-armed, bare-headed, hairy man again pointed emphatically up the mountain on the other side, and then wheeled on his heel, entered, and closed the door.

The interview had evidently not been a satis-factory one, or a friendly one to the officer, and he led his men slowly down the creek with their heads bent down intently to the trail. They did not go far. There were no fresh tracks in the way. The recent great rain had made the ground soft, and there was no mistaking the absence of the signs.

There was a consultation: three heads in broad hats close together as they could get sitting on their mules. Now a hat would be pushed back, and a face lifted up exactly in our direction. We had

sheltered behind the pines.   Klamat was holding
the Prince's mule's nose to keep it from braying to
those below.   Paquita had dismounted a little way
off, behind a clump of pines, and was plucking some
leaves and grasses for her pony and the pack-mule
to keep them still.   The Doctor never seemed more
stupid and helpless than now, but, at a sign from
Klamat, stole out to the shelter where Paquita
stood, dismounted, and began to gather grasses,
too, for his mule.

A poor, crooked, imitative little monkey he
looked as he bent to pluck the grass; at the same
time watching Paquita, as if he wished to forget
that there was any graver task on hand than to
pluck grass and feed the little mules.

Mules are noisy of a morning when they first set
out.   The utmost care was necessary now to insure
silence.

Had the wind blown in our direction, or even a
mule brayed below, these mules in the midst of our
party would have turned their heads down hill,
pointed their opera-glasses sharply for a moment or
two at the sounds below, and then, in spite of kicks
or clubs, have brayed like trumpets, and betrayed
us where we stood.

There was no excitement in the face of the Prince,

not much concern.   His foot played and patted in
the great wooden stirrup, and shook and jingled
the bells of steel on his Spanish spur, but he said
nothing.

Sometimes the men below would point in this
direction, and then in that, with their long yellow
gauntlets; then they would prick and spur their
mules till they spun round like tops.

When a man pricks and spurs his mule, you may
be sure that he is bothered.

A Yankee would scratch his head, pull at his ear,
or rub his chin; an Englishman would take snuff; a
Missourian would take a chew of tobacco, and
perhaps swear; but a Californian in the mountains
disdains to do anything so stupid and inexpressive.
He kicks and cuffs and spurs his mule.

At length the leader set his spurs in the broad
hair-sinch, with the long steel points of the rowels,
and rode down to the water's edge.   A twig was
broken there.   The Doctor had done that as we
crossed, to get a switch for his mule, and brought
down the wrath of Klamat, expressed, however,
only in frightful grimaces, signs, and the flashing of
his eyes.   The officer dismounted, leaned over,
brushed the burs aside, took some of them up, and
examined them closely.

An arm was now lifted and waved authoritatively to the two men sitting on their mules in the trail, and they instantly struck the spurs in the broad sinch, and through into the tough skins of their mules, I think, for they ambled down toward the officer at a rapid pace and — consternation! One of them threw up his head and brayed as if for life.

The Prince's mule pointed his opera-glasses, set out his legs, took in a long breath, and was just about to make the forest ring, when his master sprung to the ground, caught him by the nose, and wrenched him around till he fell upon his haunches.

Here Klamat made a sign, threw the Doctor on his mule, left Paquita to take care of herself, and led off up the hill. We mounted, and followed as fast as possible; but the Prince's mule, as if in revenge, now stopped short, set out his legs, lifted his nose, and brayed till the very pine-quills quivered overhead.

After he had brayed to his satisfaction, he gave a sort of grunt, as if to say, " We are even now," and shot ahead. The little pack-mule was no trouble. He had but a light load, and, as if in gratitude, faithfully kept his place.

A pony or horse must be led. Anything but a mule will roam and run against trees, will lodge his pack in the boughs that hang low overhead, or, worse still, stop to eat of the branches or weeds, and grasses under foot. The patient, cunning little Mexican mule will do nothing of the sort. He would starve rather than stop to eat when on duty; and would as soon think of throwing himself down over one of the cliffs that he is familiar with as to injure or imperil the pack that has been trusted to his care, by butting against trees, or lodging under the boughs that hang above the trail. He stops the instant the pack is loose, or anything falls to the ground, and refuses to move till all is made right.

We could not keep pace with Klamat, hasten as we might, through the pines. Like a spirit, he darted here and there through the trees, urging and beckoning all the time for us to follow faster.

We could not see our pursuers now, yet we knew too well that they were climbing, fast as their strong-limbed sturdy mules would serve them, the hill that we had climbed an hour before. The advantage, on one hand, was theirs; on the other, we had things somewhat our own way. The chances were about evenly balanced for escape without blood.

Any one who frequents the mountains of the North will soon notice that on all the hillsides facing the sun there is no undergrowth. You may ride there, provided you do not wedge in between the trees that grow too close together to let you pass, or go under a hanging bough, the same as in a park. But if you get on the north side of the hill, you find an under- growth that is almost impassable for man or beast. Chaparral, manzanita, madrona, plum, white thorn, and many other kinds of shrubs and trees, contribute to make a perfectly safe retreat from men for the wild beasts of those regions. In a flight, this is the chief thing to do. Keep your eye on the lay of the hills, so that you may always be on the south side, or you will find yourself in a net.

CHAPTER XVI.

ANOTHER danger lies in getting too low down on the hillside to the sea. On that side, where only grass has grown and pine-quills fallen without any undergrowth to hold them there, and contribute its own decaying and cast-off clothes to the soil, the ground is often broken, and, unlike the north side of the hills, shows here and there steep bluffs and impassable basaltic blocks, or slides of slate or shale on which it would be madness to venture.

The only safe thing to do is to find the summit, and keep along the backbone of the mountain, and thus escape the chaparral nets of the north and precipices of the south.

Great skill consists in being able to reach the summit successfully, and still greater in keeping along the backbone when it is once reached, and not follow off on one of the spurs that often shoot up higher than the back of the main ridge. There are many trails here, made by game going to and fro in the warm summer days, or in crossing the ridges

(156)

in their semi-annual migrations down to the rivers
and back again to the mountains.

The temptations to take one of these trails and
abandon the proper one, which is often dim and
sometimes wholly indistinct, are many.   It takes
the shrewdest mountaineer to keep even so much
as for one day's journey along the backbone without
once being led aside down the spurs into the nets of
chaparral, or above the impassable crags and precipices.   Of course, when you can retrace your steps
it is a matter of no great moment; you will only
lose your time.   But with us there was no going
back.

When we had reached the second bench we
turned to look.   Soon the heads of the men were
seen to shoot above the rim of the bench below;
perhaps less than a mile away.   No doubt they
caught sight of us now, for the hand of the officer
lifted, pointed in this direction, and he settled his
spurs in his sinch, and led his men in pursuit.

Deliberately the Prince dismounted, set his saddle well forward, and drew the sinch tight as possible.

We all did the same; mounted then, and followed
the boy, who had by this time set both arms
free from the odious red shirt which was now belted

about his waist, up the hill as fast as we could follow.

We reached the summit of the ridge. Scintillations from the flashing snows of Mount Shasta shimmered through the trees, and a breath of air came across from the Klamat lakes and the Modoc lands beyond, as if to welcome us from the dark, deep cañon with its leaden fringe, and lining of dark and eternal green.

The Doctor pushed his hat back from his brow and faintly smiled. He was about to kiss his hand to the splendid and majestic mountain showing in bars and sections through the trees, but looked around, caught the eye of Klamat, and his hand fell timidly to his side.

As for Paquita, she leaped from her pony and put out her arms toward her childhood home. Her face was radiant with delight. Beautiful with divine beauty, she arched her hand above her brow, looked long and earnestly at the mountain, and then, in a wild and unaccountable sort of ecstacy, turned suddenly, threw her arms about her pony's neck, embraced him passionately and kissed his tawny nose.

We had been buried in that cañon for so long, we were like men who had issued from a tomb. .As

We Could Not Keep Pace with Klamat, Hasten as We Might.

for myself, I was much as usual; I clasped and
twisted my hands together as I let my reins fall on
my horse's neck, and said nothing.

Our animals were mute now, too; no mule of the
party could have been induced to bray.   They were
tired, dripping with sweat, and held their brown
noses low and close to the ground, without attempting to touch the weeds or grasses.

Suddenly Klamat threw up his hand.   The men
had appeared on the bench below.   But we had
evidently gained on them considerably, for here we
had ten minutes' rest before they broke over the
mountain bench beneath.   This was encouraging.
No doubt a saddle had slipped off back over a
mule's rump in some steep place, and thus caused
the delay, for they had neglected to sinch their saddles in their great haste.

They dismounted now, and settled their saddles
again.   We tightened our saddles also.

When the officer threw his leg over the macheers
of his saddle below, Klamat set forward.   His skill
was as wonderful as his endurance.   Being now on
the summit, he could travel without halting to
breathe; this, of course, would be required if he
hoped to keep ahead.   And, even then, where
would it all end?   It is most likely no one had

thought of that.   For my part, I kept watching the
sun and wishing for night.

There is an instinctive desire of all things rational
or irrational, I think, that are compelled to fly, to
wish for night.

"O that night or Blucher would come."

It was hardly possible to keep ahead of our pursuers all day, well mounted as they were, and one
of our party on foot, yet that seemed to be the only
hope.   There yet was an alternative, if the worst
came to the worst.   We could ambush and shoot
them down.   I saw that Klamat kept an eye constantly on his rifle when not foxing the trail and
eying the pursuers.

The Prince was well armed.   He carried his
double-barreled piece before him in the saddle-
bow.   The rest of us were not defenseless.   The
deed was more than possible.

These men wanted the Doctor: him only, so far as
we knew.   The Doctor was accused of murder.
The officer, no doubt, had due process and the
legal authority to take him.   To the Prince he was
nothing much.   He was no equal in physical or
mental capacity.   He was failing in health and in
strength, and could surely be of no future possible

use to us. Why should the Prince take life, or even imperil ours, for his sake?

The answer, no doubt, would be very unsatisfactory to the civilized world, but it was enough for the Prince. The man needed his help. The man was almost helpless. This, perhaps, was the first and strongest reason for his course.

But at the bottom of all other reasons for taking care of this man, who seemed to become every day less capable of taking care of himself, was a little poetical fact not forgotten. This man furnished bread when we were hungry — when the snow was deep, when the earth lay in a lock-jaw, as it were, and could not open her mouth to us.

Now and then Klamat would turn his eyes over his shoulder, toss his head, and urge on. The eagle-feathers in his black hair, as if glad to get back again in the winds of Shasta, floated and flew back at us, and we followed as if we followed a banner. A black banner this we followed, made of the feathers of a fierce and bloody bird. Where would it lead us? No buccaneers of the sea were freer, wilder, braver at heart than we. Where would it lead us?

One thing was fearfully against us. The recent rains had made the ground soft and spongy. The

11

four horses made a trail that could be followed on the run. Even where the pine-quills lay thickest, the ground would be broken here and there so as to leave little doubt or difficulty to our pursuers.

Had it been a dry autumn the ground would have been hard as an adobe, and we might have dodged to one side almost anywhere, and, providing our mules did not smell and hail the passing party, escaped with impunity. As it was, nothing seemed left but to persist in flight to the uttermost. And this we did.

We did not taste food. We had not tasted water since sunrise, and it was now far in the afternoon. The Doctor began to sit with an unsteady motion in his saddle. The mules were beginning to bray; this time from distress, and not excess of spirits. The Prince's mule had his tongue hanging out between his teeth, and, what was worse, his ears began to flop to and fro as if they had wilted in the sun. Some mules put their tongues out through their teeth and go very well for days after; but when a mule lets his ears swing, he has lost his ambition, and is not to be depended on much longer.

A good mountain mule should not tire short of a week, but there is human nature wherever there is a bargain to be made, and there are mule jockeys as well as horse jockeys even in the mountains; and you cannot pick up good mules when you like, either for love or money. The men who followed had, no doubt, a tried and trusty stock. Things began to look critical.

The only thing that seemed unaffected was Klamat. Our banner of eagle feathers still floated defiantly, and promised to lead even further than we could follow. Closer and closer came the pursuers. We could see them striking their steel spurs in their sinches as if they would lift their tired mules along with their heels.

Once they were almost within hail; but a saddle slipped, and they lost at least ten minutes with a fractious mule, that for a time concluded not to be sinched again till it had taken rest.

The sugar-pines dropped their rich and delicate nuts as we rode by, from pyramid cones as long as your arm, and little foxy-looking pine squirrels with pink eyes stopped from their work of hoarding them for winter, to look or chatter at us as we hurried breathless and wearily past.

Mount Shasta still flashed down upon us through the dark, rich boughs of fir and pine, but did not thrill us now.

When the body is tired, the mind is tired too.
You get surfeited with grandeur at such a time.
No doubt the presence tames you somewhat, tones
down the rugged points in you that would like to
find expression; that would find expression in
feeble words but for this greatness which shows
you how small you are; but you are subdued rather
than elevated.

Suddenly Klamat led off to the right as if for-
saking the main summit for a spur. This seemed
a bad sign. The Prince said nothing. At any
other time, I daresay, he would have protested.

We had no time to dispute now; besides, almost
any change from this toilsome and eternal run was
a relief. What made things seem worse, however,
this boy seemed to be leading us back again to The
Forks. We were edging around at right angles
with our pursuers. They could cut across if we
kept on, and head us off. We were making more
than a crescent; the boy was leading us right back
to the men we wished to escape.

Soon he went out on a point and stopped. He
beckoned us to ride up. We did so. It seemed
less than half a mile to a point we had passed an
hour since, and, as far as we could see, there was
only a slight depression between. The officer and

his party soon came in sight. As they did so, he raised his arm. We were not unobserved.

Klamat sat down to rest, and made signs that we should dismount. I looked at the Prince to see what he would do. He swung himself to the ground, looking tired and impatient, and we all did the same. The Doctor could not keep his feet, but lay down, helpless, on the brown bed of quills from the sugar-pines that clustered around and crowned the point where we had stopped to rest.

The officer and his men looked to their catenas; each drew a pistol, revolved the cylinder, settled the powder back in the tubes by striking the ivory handles gently on the saddle pommels, saw that each nipple still held its cap, and then spurred his mule down the hillside as if to cross the depression that lay between, and head us off at once.

They were almost within hail, and I thought I could hear the clean, sharp click of the steel bells on their Spanish spurs as they descended and disappeared among the tree-tops as if going down into a sea.

Klamat had learned some comic things in camp, even though he had not learned, or pretended he had not learned, to talk. When the men had disappeared among the branches of the trees, he turned to the Prince and gravely lifted his thumb to his nose, elevated his fingers in the air, and wriggled them in the direction of the place where the officer was seen to descend.

Every moment I expected to see the muzzles of those pistols thrust up through the pines. They did not appear, however, and, as we arose to adjust our saddles after some time, I stepped to the rim of the hill and looked over to the north side. The hill was steep and rugged, with a ledge, and lined with chaparral. A white-tailed rabbit came through, sat down, and looked back into the cañon. Some quails started and flew to one side, but that was all I saw or heard.

The Doctor had now to be assisted to his saddle. He was pale, and his lips were parched and swollen. Slowly now Klamat walked ahead ; he, too, was tired. We had rested too long, perhaps. You cannot get an Indian to sit down when on a long and severe journey, unless compelled to, to rest others. The cold and damp creeps into the joints, and you get stiff and tenfold more tired than before. Great as the temptation is to rest, you should first finish your whole day's journey before you let your nerves relax.

Slowly as we moved, however, our pursuers did

not reappear. We were still on the ridge, in spite of the sharp and eccentric turn it had taken around the head of the river.

As the sun went down, broad, blood-red banners ran up to the top of Shasta, and streamed away to the south in hues of gold; streamed and streamed as if to embrace the universe in one great union beneath one banner. Then the night came down as suddenly on the world as the swoop of an eagle.

The Doctor, who had all the afternoon kept an uncertain seat, now leaned over on his mule's mane, and had fallen, but for the Prince who was riding at his side.

Klamat came back and set his rifle against a pine. We laid the feeble man on the bed of quills, loosened the sinches as the mules and ponies let their noses droop almost to the ground, and prepared to spend the night.

A severe ride in the mountains at any time is a task. Your neck is wrenched, and your limbs are weary as you leap this log or tumble and stumble your tired animal over this pile of rocks or through that sink of mud, until you are tired enough by night; but when you ride an awkward and untrained mule, when you have not sat a horse for a

year, and have an old saddle that fits you like an
umbrella or a barrel, you get tired, stiff-limbed, and
used up in a way that is indescribable. As for
poor Paquita, she was literally crucified, but went
about picking up quills for beds for all, and never
once murmured.

The Doctor was very ill.   Klamat went down the
hillside and found some water to wet his lips, but
this did not revive him.   It was a cold evening.
The wind came pitching down from Shasta, sharp
and sudden.

We spread a bed for the suffering man, but still
he shivered and shook, and we could not get him
warm.   We, too, were suffering from the cold.
We could hardly move when we had rested a
moment and let the wind drive the chill to the
marrow.

" A fire," said the Prince.

Klamat protested against it.   The sick man grew
worse.   Something warm would restore him.

We must have a fire.   Paquita gathered up some
pine knots from the hillside.   A match was struck
in the quills.   The mules started, lifted their noses,
but hardly moved as the fire sprung up like a giant
full-grown, and reached for the cones of the sugar-
pines overhead.   There was comfort and compan-

ionship in the fire. We could see each other now, —our little colony of pilgrims. We looked at one another and were revived.

We had a little coffee-pot, black and battered it is true, but the water boiled just the same, and as soon as if it had been silver.

This revived the Doctor. Hunger had much to do with his faintness. He now sat up and talked, in his low, quiet way, looking into the fire and brushing the little mites of dust and pine quills from his shirt, as if still to retain his great respectability of dress; and by the time we had all finished our coffee, he was almost as cheerful as we had ever seen him before.

The moon came out clear and cold, and we spread our blankets on the quills between the pines, with the snowy front of Shasta lifting — lifting like a bank of clouds away to the left, and the heads of many mining streams dipping away in so many wild and dubious directions, that no one but our little leader, perhaps, could have found the way through without the gravest embarrassment.

" Lie down, Paquita," said the Prince; " lie down and rest with your moccasins to the fire; you have had a hard and bitter day of it. I will keep the fire."

The child obeyed.   He waved his hand at me to do the same, and I was soon sound asleep.

The last I saw of the Prince before falling asleep, he was resting on his side with his hand on his head, and elbow on his blankets.   In the mountains, when you spread your blankets, you put your arms —rifle or pistols—in between the blankets as carefully as if they were children.   This is done, in the first place, to keep them dry, and, in the second place, to have them ready for use.   They are laid close to your side.   The heat of your body keeps out the damp.

I awoke soon.   I was too bruised, and sore, and sick in mind and body, to sleep.   There is a doleful, dreary bird that calls in this country in the night, in the most mournful tone you can imagine. It is a sort of white-headed owl; not large, but with a very hoarse and coarse note.   One of these birds was calling at intervals down the gorge to the right, and another answered on the other side so faintly I could just hear it.   An answer would come just as regularly as this one called, and that would sound even more doleful and dreary still, because so far and indistinct.   The moon hung cold and crooked overhead, and fell in flakes through the trees like snow.

But we were safe now in the strong, dark arms of mother night. Our pursuers were lost in the sea of pines below.

CHAPTER XVII.

HOME.

A PECULIARLY nervous man suffers from a mental ailment as distinctly as from a wound. He grows weak under the sense of mental distress the same as an ordinary man does from the loss of blood. Remove the cause of apprehension, and he recovers the same as the wounded man recovers. Free the mind, and you stop the flow of blood. He grows strong again.

We moved on a little way the next day, slowly, to be sure, but fast enough and far enough to be able to pitch our camp in a place of our own choosing, with wood, water and grass, the indispensable requisites of a mountain camp, all close at hand.

To the astonishment of all, the Doctor unsaddled his mule, gathered up wood, and was a full half-hand at supper. At night he spread his own blankets, looked to his pistols like an old mountaineer, and seemed to be at last getting in earnest with life. The next day, as we rode through the trees, he whistled at the partridges as they ran in strings across the trails, and chirped at the squirrels overhead.

How delightful it was to ride through the grass and trees, hear the partridges whistle; pack and unpack the horses, pitch the tent by the water, and make a military camp, and talk of war; imagine battles, shooting from behind the pines, and always, of course, making yourself a hero. Splendid! I was busy as a bee. I cooked, packed, stood guard, killed game, did everything. And so we journeyed on through the splendid forests, under the awful, frowning front of Shasta, and over peaceful little streams that wound silently through the grass, as if afraid, till we came to the headwaters of the Sacramento.

Sometimes we saw other camps. White tents pitched down by the shining river, among the scattered pines; brown mules and spotted ponies feeding and half buried in the long grass; and the sound of the picks in the bar below us — all made a picture in my life to love.

Once we fell in with an Indian party — pretty girls and lively, unsuspicious boys, along with their parents — fishing for salmon, and not altogether at war with the whites. They treated us with great kindness.

At last we branched off entirely to ourselves, cut-
ting deep into the mountain as the winter approached,
looking for a home. The weak condition of the
Doctor made it necessary that we bring our
journey to a close. We had taken a different route
from others, for good and sufficient reasons. The
trails and tracks of the hundreds of gold-hunters,
who had mostly preceded us some months, lay considerably west of Mount Shasta, striking the head
of the Sacramento River at its very source. They
had found only a few placers with float gold, not in
sufficient quantities to warrant the location of a
camp, and pushed on to the mines farther south.

We sometimes met a party of ten or more, all
well armed and mounted, ready to fight or fly as
the case might require. The usual mountain civili-
ties would be exchanged, brief and brusque enough,
and each party would pass on its way, with a frequent glance thrown back suspiciously at our Indian
boy with his rifle, the invalid Doctor leaning on his
catenas, the Indian girl with her splendid hair and
face as bright as the morning, and the majestic
figure of the Prince. An odd-looking party was
ours, I confess.

Paquita knew every dimple, bend, or spur in
these mountains now. The Prince intrusted her

to select some suitable place to rest. One evening she drew rein and reached out her hand. Klamat stood his rifle against a pine, and began to unpack the tired little mule, and all dismounted without a word.

It was early sundown. A balm and a calm was on and in all things. The very atmosphere was still as a shadow and seemed to say, " Rest, rest! " We were on the edge of an opening; a little prairie of a thousand acres, inclining south, with tall, very tall grass, and a little stream straying from where we were to wander through the meadow. A wall of pines stood thick and strong around our little Eden, and, when we had unsaddled our tired animals and taken the apparajo from the little packer, we turned them loose in the little Paradise, without even so much as a lariat or hackamoor to restrain them.

The sun had just retired from the body of the mountain, but it was evident that all day long he rested here and made glad the earth; for crickets sang in the grass as they sing under the hearthstones in the cabins of the West, and little birds started up from the edge of the valley that were not to be found in the forest.

An elk came out from the fringe of the wood,

threw his antlers back on his shoulders, with his
brown nose lifted, and blew a blast as he turned to
fly that made the horses jerk their heads from the
grass, and start and wheel around with fright.   A
brown deer came out, too, as if to take a walk in
the meadow beneath the moon, but snuffed a breath
from the intruders and turned away.   Bears came
out two by two in single file, but did not seem to
notice us.

Some men say that the bear is deprived of the
sense of smell in the wild state.   A mistake.   He
relies as much on his nose as the deer; perhaps
more, for his little black eyes are so small that they
surely are not equal to the great liquid eyes of the
buck, which are so set in his head that he may see
far and wide at once.   But the bear carries his
nose close to the ground, and of course can hardly
smell an intruder in his domains until he comes
upon his track.   Then it is curious to observe him.
He throws himself on his hind legs, stands up tall
as a man, thrusts out his nose, lifts it, snuffs the air,
turns all around in his tracks, and looks and smells
in every direction for his enemy.   If he is a cub,
however, or even a cowardly grown bear, he
wheels about the moment he comes upon the track,

will not cross it under any circumstances, and plunges again into the thicket.

We had a blazing fire soon, and at last, when we had sat down to the mountain meal, spread on a canvas mantaro, each man on his saddle or a roll of blankets, with his knife in hand, Klamat looked at our limited supply of provisions, and then pointed to the game in the meadow.

He pictured sunrise, the hunt, the deer, the crack of his rifle, and how he would come into camp laden with supplies. All this, he gave us to understand, would take place to-morrow, as he placed a sandwich between his teeth, and threw his eyes across his shoulder at the dark figures stealing through the grass across the other side of our little Eden.

The morning witnessed the fulfillment. Paquita was more than busy all day in dressing venison, and drying the meat for winter. The place was as full of game as a park. No lonelier or more isolated place than this on earth. We walked about and viewed our new estates. The mules and ponies rolled in the rich grass, or rested in the sun with drooping heads and half-closed eyes.

Even the invalid Doctor seemed to revive in a most sudden and marvelous way. He saw that no

white man's foot had ever trod the grasses of this
valley; that there we might rest and rest, and
never rise up from fear.   He could trust the wall
of pine that environed us.   It was impassable.   He
stood before an alder-tree that leaned across the
babbling, crooked little stream, and with his sheath-
knife cut this word — HOME.

A little way from here Paquita showed us another
opening in the forest.   This was a wider valley,
with warm sulphur and soda springs in a great crescent all around the upper rim.   Here the elk would
come to winter, she said; and here we could never
want for meat.   The earth and atmosphere were
kept warm here from the eternal springs; and grass
would be fresh and green the winter through.

So here we built our cabin, reared a fortress
against the approaching winter without delay, for
every night his sentries were coming down bolder
and bolder about the camp.

This was the famous " Lost Cabin. "   It stood on
a hillside, a little above the prairie, facing the sun,
close to the warm springs, and was not unlike an
ordinary miner's cabin, except that the fireplace
was in the center of the room instead of being
awkwardly placed at one end, where but few can

get the benefit of the fire. This departure was not without reason.

In the first place, the two Indians, constituting nearly half of the voting population of our little colony, insisted on it with a zeal that was certainly commendable; and, as they insisted on nothing else, it was only justice to listen to them in this.

" By-and-by my people will come," said Paquita, " and then you will want an Indian fire, a fire that they can sit down by and around without sending somebody back in the cold."

No Indian had as yet, so far as we knew, discovered us. Paquita had from the first, around the fire, told her plans; how that, as soon as she should be well rested from her journey, and a house was built and meat secured for the winter, she would take her pony, strike a trail that lay still deeper in the woods, and follow it up till she came to her father's winter lodges.

How enthusiastically she pictured the reception. How clearly she pictured it all. She would ride into the village at sundown, alone; the dogs would bark a great deal at her red dress. Then she would dismount, and go straight up to her father's lodge, and sit down by the door. The Indians would pass by and pretend not to see her, but all the time

be looking slyly sideways, half-dead to know who
she was. Then, after a while, some one of the
women would come out and bring her some water.
Maybe that would be her sister. If it was her
sister, she would lift up her left arm, and show her
the three little marks on the wrist, and then they
would know her.

One fine morning she set forth on her contem-
plated journey. I did not like the place so well
now. The forest was black, gloomy, ghostly — a
thing to be dreaded. Before, it was dreamy, deep ·
—a marvel, a something to love and delight in.
The cabin, that had been a very palace, was now
so small and narrow, it seemed I would suffocate
in the smoke; The fires did not burn so well as
they did before. Nobody could build a fire like
Paquita.

Back from our cabin a little way were some grand
old bluffs, topped with pine and cedar, from which
the view of valley, forest, and mountain, was all
that could be desired. A little way down the
waters of the valley came together, and went
plunging all afoam down the cañon, almost impassable, even for footmen. Here we found fine veins
of quartz, and first-rate indications of gold, both in
the rock and in the placer. The Prince and the

Doctor revived their theories on the origin of gold, and had many plans for putting their speculations to the test.

Klamat was never idle, yet he was never social. There was a bitterness, a sort of savage deviltry, in all he did. A fierce, positive nature was his, and hardly bridled.

Whether that disposition dated further back than a certain winter, when the dead were heaped up, and the wigwams burned, on the banks of the Klamat, or whether it was born there of the blood and bodies in the snow, and came to life only when a little, naked skeleton savage sprung up in the midst of men with a club, I do not pretend to say, but I should guess the latter. I can picture him a little boy, with bow and arrows, not over gentle it is true, but, still, a patient little savage, like the rest, talking and taking part in the sports, like those around him. Now, he was prematurely old. He never laughed; never so much as smiled; took no delight in anything, and yet refused to complain. He did his part, but kept his secrets and his sorrows to himself, whatever they may have been.

Klamat had never alluded to the massacre in any way whatever. Once, when it was mentioned, he turned his head and pretended not to hear. Yet,

somehow it seemed to me that that scene was before
him every moment.   He saw it in the fire at night,
in the forest by day.   There are natures that cannot forget if they would.   A scene like that settles
down in the mind; it takes up its abode there and
refuses to go away.

Indians in the aggregate forget less than any other
people.   They remember the least kindness perfectly well all through life, and a deep wrong is as
difficult to forget.   The reason is, I should say,
because the Indian does not meet with a great deal
of kindness as he goes through life.   His mind and
memory are hardly overtaxed, I think, in remem-
bering good deeds from the white man.

Besides, their lives are very monotonous.   But
few events occur of importance outside their wars.
They have no commercial speculations to call off the
mind in that direction; no books to forget themselves in, and cannot go beyond the sea, and hide
in old cities, to escape any great sorrow that pur-
sues them.   So they have learned to remember the
good and the bad better than do their enemies.

CHAPTER XVIII.

THE LOST CABIN.

THE snow began to fall, and Paquita did not return.

Elk came down the mountain toward the spring, and we could shoot them from our cabin door. At this season of the year, as well as late in the fall, they are found in herds of hundreds together.

It seems odd to say that they should go up further into the mountains as winter approaches, instead of down into the foot-hills and plains below, as do the deer, but it is true. There are warm springs — in fact, all mountain springs are warmer in the winter than in the summer — up the mountain, where vine-maple, a kind of watercress, and swamp briars grow in the warm marshes or on the edges, and here the elk subsist. When the maple and grasses of one marsh are consumed, they break through the snow in single file, led in turns by the bulls, to another.

Hundreds in this way make but one great track, much as if a great, big log had been drawn to and fro' through the snow. The cows come up last, to protect the calves in the line of march from the wolves.

It is a mistake to suppose that elk use their splendid horns in battle. These are only used to receive the enemy upon, a sort of cluster of bay-onets in rest. All offensive action is with the feet. An elk's horns are so placed on his head, that, when his nose is lifted so as to enable him to move about or-see his enemy, they are thrown far back on his shoulders, where they are quite useless. He strikes out with his feet, and throws his head on the ground to receive his enemy. You have much to fear from the feet of an elk at battle, but nothing from his matchless antlers.

The black bears here also go up the mountain when the winter approaches. They find some hol-low trunk, usually the trunk of a sturdy tree, and creep into it close down to the ground. Here they lie till snowed in and covered over, very fat, for months and months, in a long and delightful sleep, and never come out till the snow melts away, or they have the ill-fortune to be smelled out by the Indian dogs.

Whenever Indians find a black bear thus, they pound on the tree and call to him to come out. They challenge him in all kinds of bantering language, call him a coward and a lazy, fat old fellow, that would run away from the squaws, and would sleep all summer. They tell him it is springtime now, and he had better get up and come out and see the sun. The most remarkable thing, however, is, that, so soon as the bear hears the pounding on the tree, he begins to dig and endeavor to get out; so that the Indians have but little to do, after his den is discovered, but to sit down and wait till he crawls out — blinking and blinded by the light in his small, black eyes — and dispatch him on the spot. Bears, when taken in this way, are always plump and tender, and fat as possible; a perfect mass of white, savory oil.

I sometimes think we partook somewhat of the nature of the bear, in our little snowy cabin among the firs that winter, for, before we hardly suspected it, the birds came back, and spring was fairly upon us.

When the snow had disappeared, and our horses grew sleek and fat and strong again, Klamat and I rode far into the pines together and found a lake where the wild geese built nests, in the margin among the tules.

The Prince and the Doctor went up the cañon in search of gold, for want of something better to

do, and, by the time the summer set in, had found
a rich "pocket" in a quartz ledge, up toward the
mountain top.

Paquita had not returned.   We had come almost
not to mention her now at all.   Often and often,
all through the spring and early summer, I saw the
Prince stand out as the sun went down, and shade
his brow with his hand, looking the way she had
gone.   I think it was this that kept him here so
faithfully.

The Doctor sometimes took long journeys down
toward the valley to the south, and even fell in with
white men, as well as Indians, in that direction, and
thought of going down that way out of the reach
of the snow, and building him a house for the winter.
No one objected to this; and, when he was ready to
go away, the Prince compelled him to take half the
gold they had taken from the "pocket," even against
his utmost remonstrance.

"Take it," said the Prince, " every ounce of it.
Here it is not worth that much lead."   And he put
the buckskin bag into the Doctor's catenas, and
resolutely buckled them down.

Another incident worth mentioning in the conduct of the Prince was his earnest entreaty with the
Doctor to never reveal the existence of the mine,

His reason was of the noblest kind, sufficient, above every selfish consideration.

" In the first place," said he "gold is of doubtful utility to the world at best. But if this mine is made known, a flood of people will pour in here; the game, the forests, all this wild, splendid part of nature will disappear. The white man and the red man will antagonize, the massacre of the Klamat will be repeated; and for all this, what will be the consideration?"

For my own part, I would banish gold and silver, as a commercial medium, from the face of the earth. I would abolish the use of gold and silver altogether, have paper currency, and but one currency in all the world. I would take all the strong men now in the mines down from the mountains, and build ships and cities by the sea.

These thousands of men can, at best, in a year's time, only take out a few millions of gold. A ship goes to sea and sinks with all these millions, and there all that labor is lost to the world forever. Had these millions been in paper, only a few hours' labor would have been lost. There are two hundred thousand men, the best and bravest men in the world, wasting the best years of their lives getting out this gold. They are turning over the

mountains, destroying the forests, and filling up the
rivers.   They make the land unfit even for savages.
Take them down from the mountains, throw one-half
their strength and energy against the wild, rich sea-
border of the Pacific, and we would have, instead
of those broken mountains, muddied rivers, and
ruined forests, such an Eden as has not been seen
by man since the days of Adam.

*   *   *   *   *   *   *

At last Paquita came.   The Prince went forth to
meet her with his arms held out, but she was too
bashful and beautiful to touch.

And why had she not returned before?   It is a
sad story, but soon told.

When she reached the region of her father's camp
she found the grass growing in the trails.   She
found no sisters to receive her; no woman to bring
her water; not a human being in all the lodges.
The weeds grew rank, and the wolves had possession.

The white men in her absence had made another
successful campaign against her people.   The
Indians had become dispirited, and, never over-
provident, finding the country overrun, the game
made wild and scarce, and the fish failing to come
up the muddied Sacramento, they had neglected to

prepare for winter, and so had perished by whole villages.

These singular people perish so easily from contact with the whites, that they seem to me like the ripened fruit ready to fall at the first shaking.

She had found none of her tribe till she passed away on to the Tula lakes, and then of all her family found only two brothers. These had now come with her on her return.

They dismounted, and built a fire under the trees and apart from us, and only slowly came to communicate, to smoke, and show any friendship at all. Paquita was all kindness; but she had become a woman now; the state of things was changed. Then, the eyes of her sober, savage brothers — who could ill brook the presence of the white man, much less look with favor on familiarities — were upon her, and she became a quiet, silent Indian woman, instead of the lively maiden who had frolicked on the hillsides and wandered through the woods the year before.

They remained camped here many days. Klamat took the young chiefs up to the mine — only a little crevice in the rotten quartz — and they looked at it long and curiously. Then they picked up some little pieces of gold that lay there, looked at them, put them in their mouths, spat them out, and threw them down on the ground.

After that they came down to the cabin.

" You have saved our sister," the eldest said, among other things, " and we like you for that, and owe you all that we can give; but you did not save her from a bear or a flood — you only saved her from your own people; so that is'not so much. But, even if you did save one of us in the bravest way, that is no reason why you should help to destroy us all. If you bring men and dig gold here, we must all die. We know how that is. You may stay here, dig gold, hunt, live here all your lives; but, if you let this be known, and bring men up here, we will shoot them from behind the trees, steal their horses, and destroy them every way we can."

Paquita herself repeated this, interpreted what we did not understand, and told us emphatically that what her brothers said was true.

The Prince answered very kindly and earnestly. He told them they were right. He told them that no one should hear of the mine; and, at the last, he lifted up his hand to Mount Shasta, and, before the God of the white man and the red man, promised that no white man should come there, with his con- sent, while he remained.

Paquita returned soon after this with her people to her village, and it was lonely enough to be sure. The Prince grew restless. We mounted our horses, and set out for the settlement to procure ammunition and supplies. We went by a circuitous way to avoid suspicion.

The Indian boy, our strange manner of dress, and the Prince's lavish use of money, soon excited remark and observation. New rich mines were becoming scarce, and there were hordes of men waiting eagerly in every camp for some new thing to come to the surface.

One day the Prince met a child in an immigrant camp, the first he had seen for a long time. He stopped, took from his buckskin purse a rough nugget, half quartz and half gold, gave it to the boy, patted him on the head, and passed on. A very foolish thing.

After obtaining our supplies, we set out to return. The evening of the last day in the settlement we camped under the trees by a creek, close by some prospectors, who came into our camp after the blankets were spread, and sat about the fire cursing their hard luck; long-haired, dirty-habited, and ugly-looking men they were. One was a sickly-looking man, a singularly tall, pale man, who had

but little to say. There was some gold left. It was
of no possible use to us. The Prince took him to
one side, gave him the purse, and told him to take
it and go home. Another extremely silly thing.
This man, meaning no harm of course, could not
keep the secret of the few hundred dollars' worth of
gold dust, and soon the whole affair, wonderfully
magnified too, was blown all over the country.

When we found we were being followed, we led
a sorry race indeed, and went in all directions.
Klamat entered into the spirit of it, and played
some strange forest tricks on the poor prospectors.

We eluded them all at last, and reached the cabin.
But we had laid the foundation for many a mountain tale and venture.

What extravagant tales were told! There was a
perfect army of us —half Indians, half white men.
Our horses were shod backward — an old story.
Then, again, our horses' feet were bound up in
gunny-bags, so as to leave no track. An impossible thing, for a horse will not take a single step
with his feet in muffles. To this day men still
search the Sierras for "the Lost Cabin."

CHAPTER XIX.

GOOD-BYE.

WE received a visit from the chief of the Shastas on our return. He was not a tall man, as one would suppose who had seen his warriors, but a giant in strength. You would have said, surely this man is part grizzly bear. He was bearded like a prophet.

I now began to spend days and even weeks in an Indian village over toward the south in a cañon, to take part in the sports of the young men, listen to the teachings and tales of the old, and was not unhappy.

The Prince was losing his old cheerfulness as the summer advanced, and once or twice he half hinted of taking a long journey away to the world below.

At such times I would so wish to ask him where was his home, and why he had left it, but could not summon courage. As for myself, let it be here understood, once for all, that, when a man once casts his lot in with the Indians, he need return to his friends no more, unless he has grown so

13   (193)

strong of soul that he does not need their countenance, for he is, with them, disgraced forever. I
had crossed the Rubicon.

It was the time of the Autumn Feasts, when the
Indians meet together on a high oak plain, a
sort of hem of the mountain, overlooking the far
valley of the Sacramento, to celebrate the season
in dance and song, and recount the virtues of
their dead. On this spot, among the oaks, their
fathers had met for many and many a generation.
Here all were expected to come in rich and gay
attire, and to give themselves up to feasting and
the dance, and show no care in their faces, no
matter how hard fortune had been upon them.

Indian summer, this. A mellowness and balm in
all the atmosphere; a haze hanging over all things,
and all things still and dreamful like, like a summer sunset.

The manzanita berries were yellow as gold, the
rich anther was here, the maple and the dogwood
· that fringed the edge of the plain were red as scarlet, and set against the wall of firs in their dark,
eternal green.

The scene of the feast was a day's ride from the
cabin, and the Prince and I were expected to attend. Paquita would, of course, be there, and who

shall say we had not both looked forward to this day with eagerness and delight?

We went to the feast — rode through the forest in a sort of dream. How lovely! The deer were going in long bands down their worn paths to the plains below, away from the approaching winter. The black bears were fat and indolent, and fairly shone in their rich, oily coats, as they crossed the trail before us.

Hundreds were at the feast, and we were more than welcome. The chief came first, his warriors by his side, to give us the pipe of peace and welcome, and then a great circle gathered around the fire, seated on their robes and the leaves; and, as the pipe went round, the brown girls danced gay and beautiful, half nude, in their rich black hair and flowing robes.

But Paquita was shy. She would not dance, for somehow she seemed to consider that this was a kind of savage entertainment, and out of place for her. She had seen just enough of civilized life to deprive her of the pleasures of the wild and free.

There had grown a cast of care upon her lovely face of late. She was in the secret of all the Indians' plans. At least she was a 'true Indian —

true to the rights of her race, and fully awake to a
sense of their wrongs.

She was surely lovelier now than ever before; tall,
and lithe, and graceful as a mountain lily swayed by
the breath of morning. On her face, through the
tint of brown, lay the blush and flush of maiden-
hood, the indescribable sacred something that makes
a maiden holy to every man of manly nature. There
is a love that makes a man utterly unselfish, and
perfectly content to love and be silent, to worship
at a distance, as turning to the holy shrine of
Mecca, to be still and bide his time; caring not to
possess in the low, coarse way that characterizes
your common lover of to-day, but choosing, rather,
to go to battle for her — bearing her in his heart
through many lands, through storms, and on down
to the doors of death, with only a word of hope, a
smile, a wave of the hand from a wall, a kiss blown
far, as he mounts his battle horse below and
plunges into the night. That is a love to live for.
I say the knights of Spain, bloody as they were,
were a noble and splendid type of men in their way.

The Prince was of this manner of men. He was
by nature a knight of the brave old days of Spain,
a hero born out of time, and blown out of place,
in the mines and mountains of the North.

Once he had taken Paquita in his arms, had folded
a robe around her as if she had been a babe.   She
was all — everything to him.   He renounced all
this.   Now he did not even touch her hand.

The old earnestness and perplexity had come
upon the Prince again on our coming to the feast.
Once, when the dance and song ran swift and loud,
and all was merriment, I saw him standing out from
the circle of warriors, of young maidens and men,
with folded arms, looking out on the land below.   I
had too much respect, nay reverence, for this man
to disturb him.   I leaned against a tree and looked
as he looked.   Once his eyes left the dance before
him, and stole timidly toward the place where
Paquita sat with her brother watching the dance.
What a devotion in his face.   I could not understand him.   Then he turned to the valley again,
tapped the ground with his foot in the old, restless
way, but his eyes soon wandered back to Paquita.
At last my gaze met his.   He blushed deeply, held
down his head and walked away in silence.

The next day was the time set apart for feats of
horsemanship.   The band of mustangs was driven
in, all common property, and the men selected their
horses.   The Prince drew out with his lasso a stout
black stud, with a neck like a bull.   His mane

poured down on either side, or stood erect like a
crest; a wiry, savage, untrained horse that struck out
with his feet, like an elk at bay. The Prince sad-
dled him, and led him out all ready now, where
the other horses stood in line, then came to me,
walked a little way to one side, put out one hand,
and with the other drew me close to him, held down
his head to my uplifted face, and said :

"Good-bye."

I sprang up and seized hold of him, but he went
on calmly :

"I must go away. You are happy here; you
will remain, but I must go. After many years I
may return. You may meet me here on this spot,
years and years from to-day. Yes, it will be
many years ; a long time. But it is short enough,
and long enough. I will forget her— it —I will
forget by that time, you see, and, then, there is all
the whole world before me to wander in."

He made the sign of departure. The chief came
forward, Paquita came and stood at his side. He
reached his hands, took her in his arms, pressed her
to his breast an instant, kissed her pure brow once,
with her great black eyes lifted to his, but said no
word.

The Indians were mute with wonder and sorrow.

When you give the sign of going, there is no one to say nay here. No one importunes you to stay; no one says come to my place or come to mine. No such folly. You know that you are welcome to one and all, and they know, that, if you · wish to go, you wish to go, and that is all there is of it. This is the highest type of politeness; the perfect hospitality.

The Prince turned to his horse, drew his red silk sash tighter about his waist, undid the lasso, wound the lariat on his arm, and wove his left hand in the flowing mane as the black horse plunged and beat the air with his feet. Then he set him back on his haunches, and sprang from the ground: then forward plunged the stud, with mane like a storm, down the place of oaks, pitching toward the valley.

The trees seemed to open rank as he passed, and then to close again; a hand was lifted, a kiss thrown back across the shoulder, and he was gone — gone down in the sea below us, and I never saw my Prince again for many a year. Noble, generous, self-denying Prince! The most splendid type of the chivalric and perfect man I had ever met.

All this was so sudden that I hardly felt the

weight of it at first, and, for want of something to
do to fill the blank that followed, I mounted my
horse and took part in the sports with the gayest
of the gay.

Indians do not speak of anything that happens suddenly. They think it over, all to themselves, for
days, unless it is a thing that requires some action
or expression at once, and they then speak of it
only cautiously and casually. It is considered very
vulgar, indeed, to give any expression to surprise,
and nothing is more out of taste than to talk about
a thing that you have not first had good time to
think about.

During the day I noticed that my catenas were
heavier than usual, and, unfastening the pockets, I
found that they contained all four of the bags of
gold.

*   *   *   *   *   *   *

Why had he left himself destitute? Why had he
gone down to battle with the world without a
shield? — gone to fight Goliath, as it were, without
so much as a little stone. I wanted to follow him,
and make him take the money—all of it. I despised
it; it made me miserable. But I had learned to obey
him — to listen to him in all things. And, was he
not a Prince?

"Ah!" said I to myself, at last, "he has gone down to take possession of his throne. He will cross the seas, and see maidens fair indeed, nearly as lovely in some respects as Paquita;" and this was my consolation.

"Years and years," I said to myself, that night, as I looked in the fire, and the dance went on; "Years and years!" I counted it upon my fingers, and said: "I will be dead then."

*   *   *   *   *   *   *

The marriage ceremony of these people is not imposing. The father gives a great feast, to which all are invited, but the bride and bridegroom do not partake of food. A new lodge is erected and furnished more elegant than any other of the village, by the women, each vying with the other to do the best in providing their simple articles of the Indian household.

In the evening, while the feast goes on, and the father's lodge is full of guests, the women and children come to the lodge with a great number of pitch torches, and two women enter and take the bride away between them; the men all the time taking no heed of what goes on. They take her to the lodge, chanting as they go, and making a great flourish with their torches. Late at night the men

rise up, and the father and mother, or those standing in their stead, take the groom between them
to the lodge, while the same flourish of torches and
chant goes on as before.   They take him into the
lodge, and set him on the robes by the bride.
This time the torches are not put out, but are laid
one after another in the center of the lodge.   And
this is the first fire of the new pair, which must
not be allowed to die out for some time.   In fact,
as a rule, in time of peace, Indians never let their
lodge-fires go out so long as they remain in one
place.

When all the torches are laid down and the fire
burns bright, they are supposed to be married.
The ceremony is over, and the company go away
in the dark.

*   *   *   *   *   *   *

Late that autumn, these Indians made the marriage feast, and at that feast neither I nor the
beautiful Indian girl took meat.

CHAPTER XX.

THE LAST OF THE LOST CABIN.

THESE Indians use but few words. A coward and a liar is the same with them ; they have no distinct terms of expressing the two sins. Sometimes a single eloquent gesture means a whole sentence, and expresses it, too, better than could a multitude of words.

I said to the old chief one day:

"Your language is very poor; it has so few words."

"We have enough. It does not take many words to tell the truth," he answered.

"Ah, but we have a hundred words to your one."

"Well, you need them."

He seemed to say, "Yes, from the number of lies you have told us, from the long treaties that meant nothing that you have made with us ; from the promises that you have made and broken, I should say that you needed even a thousand words to our one.

The old Indian arose as he said this, and gath-

ered his blanket about his shoulders.   His dog lay
with his nose on his two paws, and his eyes raised
to his master's.

" You have not words enough in all your books
to give a single look from the eyes of my dog."

He drew his blanket closer about him, turned
away, and the dog arose and followed him.

I had a pocket Bible with me once, in his camp.
I showed it to the chief, and undertook to tell him
what it was.

" It is the promise of God to man," I said, " His
written promise to us, that, if we do as He com-
manded us to do, we shall live and be happy forever when we die."

He took it in his hand, and looked at the outside
and inside very attentively.

" Promises!   Is it a treaty? "

" Well, it is a treaty, perhaps; at least, it is a
promise, and He wrote it."

" I do not like promises or long treaties.   I do
not like any treaties on paper.   They are so easy
to break.   The Indian does not want his God
to sign a paper.   He is not afraid to trust his
God."

" But the promises and the resurrection? "   I
urged.

He pointed to the new leaves on the tree, the
spears that were bursting through the ground,
handed me the book and said no more.

The Prince was gone, perhaps to never return.
I was again utterly alone with the Indians. I
looked down and out upon the world below as
looking upon a city from a tower, and was not
unhappy.

I lived now altogether with the chief.   His lodge
was my home; his family my companions.   We
rode swift horses, sailed on the little mountain
lakes with grass and tule sails, or sat down under
the trees in summer, where the wind came through
from the sea, and drank in silently the glories and
calm delights of life together.

" They will find your lost cabin yet," said the chief,
" if it is allowed to stand.   Then they will search till
they find the mine, then a crowd of people will
come, like grasshoppers in the valley ; my warriors
will be murdered, my forests cut down, my grass
will be burned, my game driven off, and my people
will starve.   As their father, to whom they look for
protection and support, I cannot allow it to stand."

" It shall be as you say.   Send some men with
me.   What care I for the cabin? and what is a mine
of gold to me here ? "

We went down, we burned the cabin to the ground.

Years afterward I passed there, and all was wild and overgrown with grass, the same as if no man had ever sat down and rested there below the boughs.

Some pines that stood too close to the burning cabin were shorn of branches on one side, and, where the bark had burned on that side, they were gnarled and seared, and stood there parched up and ugly in a circle, as if making faces at some invisible object in their midst.

*   *   *   *   *   *   *

And now, for the first time, a plan which had been forming in my mind ever since I first found myself among these people began to take definite shape. It was a bold and ambitious enterprise, and was no less a project than the establishment of a sort of Indian Republic—" a wheel within a wheel," with the grand old cone, Mount Shasta, in the midst.

To the south, reaching from far up on Mount Shasta to far down in the Sacramento Valley, lay the lands of the Shastas, with almost every variety of country and climate; to the southeast the Pitt River Indians, with a land rich with pastures, and plains teeming with game; to the northeast lay the Modocs, with lakes and pasture-lands enough to make a State.   My plan was to unite these three tribes in a confederacy under the name of the United Tribes, secure by treaty all the lands near the mountain, even if we had to surrender all the other lands in doing so.

It might have been called a kind of Indian reservation, but it was to be a reservation in its fullest and most original sense, such as those first allotted to the Indians.   Definite lines were to be drawn, and these lines were to be kept sacred.   No white man was to come there without permission.   The Indians were to remain on the land of their fathers. They were to receive no pay, no perquisites or assistance whatever from the government.   They were simply to be let alone in their possessions, with their rites, customs, religion and all, unmolested.   They were to adopt civilization by degrees and as they saw fit, and such parts of it as they chose to adopt.   They were to send a representative to the State and the national capitals if they chose, and so on through a long catalogue of details that would have left them in possession of that liberty which is as dear to the Indian as to any being on earth.

Filled with plans for my little republic, I now
went among the Modocs, whom I had always half
feared since the day they had killed and plundered
the Mexicans, and boldly laid the case before them.
They were very enthusiastic, and some of the old
councilmen named me chief; yet I never had any
authority to speak of till too late to use it to
advantage.

I drew maps and wrote out my plans, and sent
them to the commanding officer of the Pacific
Coast, the Governor of the State, and the Presi-
dent of the Republic.

The Indians entered into it with all their hearts.
Their great desire was to have a dividing line or
a mark that would say, Thus far will we come, and
no farther. They did not seem to care about
details or particularly where the line would be
drawn, only that it should be drawn, and leave
them secure in bounds which they could call their
own. They would submit to almost anything for
this.

Remove they would not ; but they were tired of
a perpetual state of half-war, half-peace, that
brought only a steady loss of life and of land, without any lookout ahead for the better, and would

enter into almost any terms that promised to let them and theirs permanently and securely alone.

How magnificent and splendid seemed my plan ! Imagination had no limit. Here would be a National Park, a place, one place in all the world, where men lived in a state of nature, and, when all the other tribes had passed away or melted into the civilization and life of the white man, here would be a people untouched, unchanged, to instruct and interest the traveler, the moralist, all men.

When the world is done gathering gold, I said, men will come to these forests to look at nature, and be thankful for the wisdom and foresight of the age that preserved this vestige of an all but extinct race. There was a grandeur in the thought, a sort of sublimity, that I shall never feel again. A fervid nature, a vivid imagination, and, above all, the matchless and magnificent scenery, the strangely silent people, the half-pathetic stillness of the forests, all conspired to lift me up into an atmosphere where the soul laughs at doubt and never dreams of failure. A shipwrecked race, I said, shall here take refuge. To the east and west, to the north and south, the busy commercial world may swell and throb and beat and battle like a sea;

14

but on this island, around this mountain, with
their backs to this bulwark, they shall look un-
troubled on it all.   Here they shall live as their
fathers lived before the newer pyramids cast their
little shadows, or camels kneeled in the dried-up
seas.

About midwinter the chief led his men up toward the higher spurs of the mountain for a great
hunt.   After some days on the headwaters of the
McCloud, at some hot springs in the heart of a deep
forest and dense undergrowth, we came upon an
immense herd of elk.   The snow was from five to
ten feet deep.   We had snow-shoes, and, as the elk
were helpless, after driving them from the thin snow
and trails about the springs into the deep snow,
the Indians shot them down as they wallowed along,
by hundreds.

Camp was now removed to this place, with the
exception of a few who preferred to remain below,
and feasting and dancing became the order of the
winter.

Soon Klamat and a few other young and spirited
Indians said they were going to visit some other
camp that lay a day or two to the east, and disappeared.

In about a month they returned.   After the usual

Indian silence, they told a tale which literally froze my blood. Indians had broken out, killed every white man in the country, captured thousands of head of stock, and restored the whole land again to their own dominion.

There were no women or children in the valley at the time of the massacre; only the men in charge of great herds of stock.

This meant a great deal to me. I began to reflect on what it would lead to. The affair, no matter who was to blame, would be called a massacre by the savages; of this I was certain. Possibly it was a massacre, but the Indian account of it shows them to have been as perfectly justified as ever one human being can be for taking the life of another.

No one has ever seemed to be willing to understand why I choose to live with the Indians instead of white people. Evil motives have forever been laid at my door because I was the only white person spared in this disaster.

I have been from that day to this charged with having led the Indians in this massacre. I deny nothing; simply tell what I know and all I know as briefly as possible, and let it pass.

CHAPTER XXI.

THE EXPEDITION.

BUT, let it be remembered, I had friends among the Indians, true and brave friends. And they are as faithful to their friends as any people on earth. Yea, let me say this now at last over the graves of these dead red men — I owe them much. I owe no white man anything at all. Looking back over the long and dubious road of my eventful life, I say this, surely I owe no white man for favor, or friendship, or lesson of love, or forbearance of any sort. Yet, to the savage red men that gathered about the base of Mount Shasta to battle and to die, I owe much — all that I am or can ever hope to be.

It seemed incredible, this massacre; it seemed utterly impossible that I should now be the only living white person in all the land. I took two faithful young Indians, and, descending almost with the rapidity of shot on our snowshoes to the flowers and green grasses of the far-off valley, I found only dead bodies and burned ruins.

Let us hasten on over the peril and the **pain**

of the tedious return through the melting snows to my own camp. Believing myself to be the first white man to learn of the massacre, I now hastened on alone to the nearest white habitation.

The fearful news had reached the city before me. I found that the editor of the paper, Mr. Irwin, afterward governor of California, and other leading men, had placed a force already in the field, and was advised to follow and use my knowledge of the country in the interests of civilization.

I thought over my plans for the Indian Republic, doubted, debated; but at last threw my energy into the expedition against the rebellious Indians. Having plenty of gold, I was soon splendidly mounted, and on my way through the snow in the track of the new troops.

Just as the stars began to glitter over the steep and stupendous walls of snow which I was now slowly climbing, I caught the cheering light of many camp fires under the somber boughs of pine and fir and cedar trees that dotted the mountain slope. My splendid horse soon had his nose in a barley bag along with others, and I broke bread with as motley a set of men as ever grouped about any camp fire on this earth. Could Shakespeare have but seen that gang! Description at my hand

would be impossible.   Perhaps twenty-five of these
men had lost brother, father, friend, fortune, in the
massacre.   These were sober and quiet enough.
Perhaps a like number had lost nothing, having had
nothing to lose, and were now merely adventurers,
on their way out to plunder the dead possibly.
Perhaps a like number were of the lowest form of
humanity; for the jails had been given a holiday.
Janus and the jail!   The old Roman deity, the
god of battles, and the Yreka mining camp in California.   .The world is round, and history keeps on
reading the same old page in tireless repetition.
Janus and the open jail!   And these men were to
be my companions through a campaign of long
and savage warfare!

CHAPTER XXII.

A MAIDEN AND A LETTER.

THE braying pack-mules, the bellowing cattle, the impatient horses pawing in the hard, deep snow, and over and above all this the yelling of wholly drunken or half-sober men, who now for the first time were confronted by the fact that they had to either cook or go hungry — all this, along with the many bright big camp-fires flashing over the mountains of snow under the dense and sable pines, made a scene Miltonic, demoniac, majestic.

To forecast the entire annihilation of this mob, calling itself the "Army of Northern California," had not been a hard task. Most of the men had pistols in their belts, but their guns leaned in hopeless neglect, wet and empty, against the pines. The Indians could easily glide in on the crusted snow from the darkness that environed us and tomahawk the last man.

But the next morning, brilliant with snow and sunlight, found the men sleeping peacefully. One by one they crawled forth from their blankets, now sunken heavily in the snow from the weight and

(215)

warmth of from two to ten half-drunken forms of
humanity, and stared hopelessly about.   The great
roaring fires of the night before had sunken deep
down in the melting snow.   Only here and there
the embers of some huge pine log still held fire
away down in the smoke-blackened pit that yawned
at the feet of the California Volunteers in their
blankets.   From under the low boughs of a dwarf
yew tree, where I, along with my horse, had spent
the night, apart from the tumultuous crowd, I could
see little groups of men gathering on the side next
toward the little city, away below the snow, and a
day's journey behind us.   These little groups would
accumulate, like rolling balls of snow, and then
break off, and silently but speedily turn their backs
on the half-awakened camp.   They had had enough
of the first great campaign against the murderous
Modocs.   There remained at informal roll-call only
two classes, the best and the worst.   The worst
cared not, or dared not, to return to prison fare,
and the best of the men who had gotten up the
sudden expedition, felt that the eyes of.the State
were on them ; besides, that they had the massacre
to avenge ; to recover lost estates ; to reclaim once
more to civilization a region as large as all New

England. These men could not desert now. But what a dismal, smoky, doughy, dreadful breakfast!

As we sat or rather stood at breakfast, a tin cup of coffee in the right hand and a sandwich of dough and burnt bacon in the other, two tall and comely Indian warriors stood over like silhouettes against the rising sun on the crest of the snowy mountain before us. Instantly I knew them for my two young friends who had gone down into the valley of death with me when we had first heard of the massacre.

Take a map and trace the route of my travel since leaving my own camp, and you will see that in three days I had made almost the entire circuit of the grandest and sublimest snow peak in all the world. I was now not forty miles from my own camp, my own Indians. These swift and splendid young fellows had kept promise, and were coming to tell me how things now stood. Their information, whatever it might be, was of the greatest importance. Did the compact with the Modocs still hold good? Were Pitt River and Modoc and Shasta still friendly? or had they quarreled over the plunder, after the fashion of white nations? All this was important to know.

But such a panic! Pistols in the air instantly! A dozen, forty, fifty shots! The two tall and

shapely figures melted back and away as they had
come.   And that was all — all except a " stampede "
of horses, cattle, mules, men! The cattle first
took fright at this apparition — those two shapely
and shadowy savages on the steep, deep snow under
the pines that lifted before us — and they, like the
men in the early morning, started for the world below!   Then the mules, madly braying, followed the
bellowing cattle.   Then the horses.   Then some
of the men dashed bravely down the mountain after
their horses.   And they never came back — cattle
horses, mules or men!

Rodgers, the banker, whose father had fallen in
the massacre, pulled the remnant of men together
that afternoon, had what few cattle butchered that
had lodged in the snow, and, as night came on and
the crust of deep snow hardened, the little band
set forward silently, slowly, in single file, through
the deep, solemn woods to cross the Sierras.   Each
man led a horse and drew a sled.   The sled was
often only the hide of a bullock, with blankets,
bread, bacon, arms, ammunition, anything indeed
that fell to the lot of the man who drew the sledge
in the general distribution of provisions.   Here
were stout, daring, audacious hearts now.   There
is not room or need to say more.   But pray give

this brave little remnant of an army tender respect. Napoleon on the Alps, the hunchback Hannibal before him, were simply luxurious robbers in comparison with this sobered and earnest little string of men on their tortuous way through the pines to recover a kingdom that had been lost to civilization. Cortez, drawing his ships by piecemeal over the isthmus, knew nothing half so terrible in that warm and luxurious land. For here with us, on the very first night, nearly every man had feet, face or hands badly frozen. And the wolves! Before it was yet quite full dawn we were compelled to form a solid circle with our faces to the wolves, our sleds and horses in the center. And such beautiful teeth! We sat down on our sleds facing the wolves. The wolves promptly sat down right before us, their great red tongues lolling out of their hungry mouths, their beautiful white teeth glistening in perilous contrast. Two sleds of beef had already been captured and instantly devoured.

"Look here! I've cut myself somehow," whispered one of the men who had lost a sled. We only discovered that he was hurt by the blood that made the white snow red. This poor fellow was reputed to be a professional pickpocket when at home in the enjoyment of civilization and liberty. But he was

a good soldier here, and did not even cry out when
a wolf tore away a handful of flesh from his leg;
but he merely laid it to some accidental awkward-
ness of his, had his leg bandaged as we all sat there,
shivering and looking down into a thousand hungry
throats, waiting, praying for sunrise.   But had that
poor pickpocket by sign or sound indicated that the
wolves had begun to eat our men as well as our
provisions, there would probably have been a two-
second panic!   Then some few white bones on the
bloody snow — the red epitaph over the common
grave of the " Army of Northern California."

When light came and the wolves went back a
little from our faces, we made roaring fires and
broiled, or rather burned, our beef, so that it would
be less heavy and, finally, less attractive to the
wolves in these terrible marches at night.   While
this was being done I posted on alone with Captain
Rodgers, whom I had come to know and greatly
respect, if not to quite yet trust, to see, if possible,
if there was any abatement in the tremendous depth
of snow, for our sleds were worn and broken, our
horses were weak and failing for want of food.
After an hour or so we crossed a huge bear track,
or, rather, what Rodgers called a bear track.   It was
simply the track of about twenty Modocs on the

war-path! They were going toward my own camp. But I kept my own counsel. There was no turning back now. To tell the worn band of men that the Modoc was also with us would have insured a sort of paralysis. It was push on now or perish.

This " bear track " at this time and place could mean but one thing — and how you need a map of the whole thing here — and that was war between the three Indian tribes that hovered about the base of Mount Shasta. Either this, or the Modocs were merely on their way to my camp for plunder. This broad bear track was pointing direct for either my camp or the scalps of my Indians. In either case the only immediate danger to the little army was the danger of a panic. But this is the most fearful danger that any man has to meet in war, especially in the wilderness, where the wild beasts, where even the elements, conspire to destroy.

Captain Rodgers sat down to rest, and I went on alone to the top of a bold and tremendous mountain of snow, from which the grasses and flowers of the desolated valley could be seen. It was here that I had rested with my two young Indians, both on going to and returning from the scene of massacre. We had left a letter here, in Indian characters, and, as these two Indians who had created the

panic before mentioned had probably passed this
way, I hoped to find a new letter from them here.
I was not disappointed. It took some patient
search, some circuitous and tedious delay, which I
have not time to set down, but this is the letter I
found on the inner side of a scale of sugar-pine
bark. Bear in mind that the sugar-pine tree is
always used by the Shasta Indians. You might
search the forest in vain for any sign on any other
tree than the sugar-pine.

To translate this letter may be tedious, but it
is absolutely necessary. In the first place, the
arrow is my name. The five dots are merely com-
plimentary adjectives, as if to say: " My five
times brave and upright and five times faithful
brother." You see these Indians never count more
than five. If they wish to say " six," they simply
say " five and one," and so on. Twenty-five is
told by saying five times five. The arrow was
given me as the sign of my name, because, as told
before, I had been dangerously shot in the face
with an arrow. The moon, dry and cold, and just
so many days old, is the date of the letter. And
now here is all the news ; and most important it
was, as you will see. The sign of the Modoc is the
reed, or rather the tule ; a long, slim line represents

THE LETTER.

the tule. This shows the early history of the Modoc on his " floating islands " among the reeds and tules of the lakes. The awkward figure, looking like a demoralized hour-glass, represents the Pitt River Indians. You see they come by this hour-glass from an immemorial custom of defending themselves against invasion by keeping a continual girdle of blind pits drawn around the edge of their vast and fertile valley. As these blind pits had sharpened elk and deer antlers at the bottom, to say nothing of deadly-pointed spears set point upward, you may well understand that they were terrible enough to give a name to any people. And do you see here the tule, or reed, although badly broken, is thrust downward entirely through the pit? You can easily read that the battle was a bloody one, and many Modocs were killed, as well as many more of their enemies.

And what does the awkward and helpless and overturned heart mean? And what is the round and helpless little circle for? Ah, me! If I were only permitted to write of that. If I had only con-tracted to write of love, and not entirely of war, in this story, then I could tell all. But surely I may be indulged to explain this tender little postscript to this thoughtful and loving letter. Briefly, then,

the year before some half hostile and wholly wild
Indians had visited my camp with a white girl, whom
they proposed to sell for two horses. The girl
could not talk to me or understand a word. She
had been a captive since a baby, and, as she did
not want to come to me, and as I would have surely
been misunderstood, I did not buy her, but waited,
hoping some white men might come my way and
help me with their presence and advice. And that
was all; I had never seen her any more. But I
had kept up constant inquiry for her, and had sent
word to Lieutenant Crook, now General Crook, and
famous in many wars, who was then in charge of
the nearest military post, of the fact about this poor
white girl prisoner. Of course, when the massacre
took place, the first question in my mind was as to
the fate of the white girl who was a prisoner among
that nomadic band of savages.

Did I forget to say that she was beautiful? Beautiful she was as any dream of beauty. She was sad
and silent, piteously sad. She stood pulling at
the tasseled tops of some tall grass at the side of
the trail, as the Indians sat on their ponies barter-
ing. That was all she did, and said nothing. She
only looked at me once, out of her great sad eyes,
that nearly all the time kept looking down. And

she did not speak, in any tongue, when I spoke to her.   And she would not come to me when I asked her to.   Nor did she give me her hand when I offered her mine.

Let the fact be at once and frankly confessed that it is doubtful if I should have gone down into the valley of death after the massacre but for the memory and the hope of this beautiful, sad and silent girl.

And this brings us back to the postscript of the Indian's letter on a bit of sugar-pine bark, which may be briefly translated thus : " As for the matter of the beautiful girl whose fate and sad fortune has quite turned your tender heart upside down, we can only say that we have learned nothing at all ; and all our search and inquiry has ended where we began: in this narrow little circle."

And now let us return to the cold and cruel page of war, and forget, so far as possible, the sad face and the great lustrous eyes that may still be seen after all these years looking out through " The Songs of the Sierras."   It is best to try to believe, that, after all, she was wholly indifferent to her condition.   If one could only think of her as a half-savage, as a Mexican girl, as anything almost but a sensitive, . sad and shrinking captive, silent from the very awe

15

and calamity of her position, from the memory of a dead mother in the grass with her babes about her, the father falling gun in hand, dying to defend her! Oh the untold tragedies written in blood on these forest leaves! Let us hasten along.

CHAPTER XXIII.

A WILD CAMPAIGN.

" LET us sacrifice to the gods, as did good old Ulysses," said Captain Rodgers that night, as we were again about to set forward in that dreadful march through the wilderness — the wolves — the snow! And, in imitation of the grand old cattle-thief of the Iliad, we laid bones, hides, all parts, indeed, that we did not want — as did old Ulysses — on the roaring log fires, as we filed past, in a long and dreary black line over and through the white snow. And, if the "savor thereof" was not "sweet to the nostrils of the gods," it certainly was pleasant to the wolves. These gaunt and ghastly creatures had already formed a circle, a slowly narrowing circle of white teeth; but the smell of roast bones and burning hides was too potent an attraction for them to abandon, and we soon had the infinite satisfaction of leaving the greater part of these shaggy and sharp-toothed creatures sitting in solemn circle around the edge of our deserted camp, their noses and long necks reaching forward. All night and all next day that weary and worn line of men struggled on in sullen silence toward the summit of the high, bald mountain, from which the great valley with its grasses and its gorgeous flowers could be seen. Sleds, horses, men, and, most important of all, even guns and ammunition, lay along that line of march almost from one end to the other. The men were too weak and worn to fight or even quarrel among themselves any more. And that is saying they were pretty weak.

A warm south wind had been soughing through the towering pines almost from the moment we set out from the camp of wolves. This singular bit of good fortune saved us, or at least many of us, from being literally eaten alive. For the warm winds and the melting snows drove the wolves back toward their haunts in the high Sierras, or at least kept them from crowding us too closely. And now we were beset by a singular bird, the garrulous magpie. This gaudy bird of gray and black and white and parti-colored plumage had been increasing in numbers from the day we first began this march through the Sierras. And now with the warm weather they were in clouds. From the first this noisy and insolent bird had sat on the backs of our pack animals where their backs were sore, and

literally eaten them alive. And now they had
grown so audacious that they would perch on even
the best of our animals, and pick at their eyes. We
had to blanket and blindfold our saddle horses to
keep them from being devoured alive by these mag-
pies. I have mentioned the fact that the winter had
been one of incredible severity, and this may account in some sort for this plague of birds, as well
as wolves, on the summit of that high, bald mountain, with the green sea of grass rolling in billows at
its base.

But how glorious was this glad face of nature,
after the long and continued and most miserable
and inglorious contact with the face of man! Never
shall I forget those far-away flowers; the perfume
of them that came up to us in the snow from their
frank and open hearts. There was a fringe of yellow on the outer line of the great green valley.
Buttercups! millions and myriads of millions of
golden buttercups! And the California poppy!
Away out in the heart of the valley, where the two
rivers, surging full from the melting snows, gathered their waters from the lakes that almost environed the valley, lay miles and miles of snow-
white hyacinths. This wild hyacinth is odorless
here, but it is perfect in its beauty. In the heart

of this wild white sea of sudden-born blossoms
slowly rose the smoke of many wigwams. The
Indians had gathered their forces and taken up
their defense on one of the many islands. This
was to be our battlefield. The plan of campaign
formed itself almost instantly in my mind, and that
feature of the work before me was dismissed. I
did not like to think of that. I had had enough of
strife, of hard and horrible enmity with man. I
wanted the flowers now. I wanted peace, rest. But
above all, I wanted to once more see the sad, sweet
face of that silent captive who had been brought to
me in my own camp only the year before. If I
could only find her, only once see her face, it seemed
to me that the hard campaign with these coarse and
brutal men could be forever remembered as a gala
day.

From my journal, kept regularly all this time,
but mostly in the Indian sign, as that was briefer,
I read that, "on the first new moon of the third
month we were camped on snow seventeen feet
deep, with flowers only four miles distant." I read
further that "on the third day of the new moon we
had four fights over my election as captain," Captain Rodgers being deposed by the popular vote of
the roughs. I, a boy, sensitive, shy, frail and

slender as a girl, was in full command of this miserable squad of humanity, with pickpockets and jail birds in the majority.

I set to work at once to descend through the fast-melting snow, and open an aggressive war even before the arrival of re-enforcements from the south.

By this time Rodgers, the deposed captain, and I had become as brothers. I told him of the war that had risen between the three tribes, to the existence of which we surely owed the preservation of this motley mob. " All Gaul is divided into three parts," said Rodgers, gayly, quoting from Cæsar in good Latin.

Does it read strangely to you that this man, here in these remote mountains, nearly forty years ago, should also have shouted out in Greek the glorious cry of the Ten Thousand when he, and he alone, stood at my side and first saw that sea of flowers below ? Well, strange or not strange, I can only tell the facts.

How bitter are the little feuds between helpless little settlements and frontier towns. And Josephus tells us that there never was in all history such hatred as arose between the followings of John and

of Simon at the time when Titus, the son of Ves-
pasian, sat down in siege around about Jerusalem.

Well, in these awful enmities, read the reason
and secret of our being able to pierce the heart of
a hostile Indian country, to cut through the heart
of the Sierras, indeed, at a time worse than mid-
winter, to sit down at the door of a brave and
powerful enemy, without firing a gun. The " three-
cornered " war among the Indians made our
approach not only possible but perfectly secure.
The Modoc was delighted to see us descend upon
the Pitt River, while he paid his attention to the
Shastas. They did not greatly dread us then. They
did not hate us half so bitterly as they hated one
another.

It was full-blown spring when we set foot among
the flowers at the base of the terrible spurs of
Mount Shasta. The men shouted with wild and
tumultuous delight. The horses, relieved of their
loads, rolled on the knee-deep grass; they threw
their weary heels in the air on the third day, and, like
the men, began to grow impatient of peace. Four
fights I find recorded for the third day. Indians
began to hover about us. They were tightening
their lines, and drawing their numbers, in increased
strength, to a solid circle, as did the wolves back

in the fearful heights of snow.   The singular good
fortune of the little army in escaping all peril thus
far, had made it insolent.   It was ambitious to do
battle before the arrival of re-enforcements.

" When will we fight these red devils ? "

" We will fight when I get ready to fight."

That night the mob held another election, and
there was a new captain.   This time the toughs
chose one of their own number, the best of their
number, it is true.   But that is not high praise of
the new captain.

We had fired a good many shots, and we had
also gathered up many arrows that had been sent
us in return.   But what the new captain most desired was not a dead, but a live Indian, one who
could tell him how near re-enforcements were, and
also tell the strength and condition of hostile camps.
And, with the capture of a live Indian in view, the
new captain, not at all a commander, signaled his
election to office by taking off his shoes and taking
after and attempting to run down and capture an
Indian with his own hand.

After that, discipline was utterly out of the question.   Besides, we were now on quarter-rations.   A
secure camp was selected and fortified, and we sat
down to wait for re-enforcements.   And while wait-

ing, and with only quarter-rations to keep up their strength, these gallant men certainly fought; fought one another ! And these battles were not entirely among the toughs, either. I had a young, fair-haired friend, a boy in fact, and the youngest of the expedition except myself. And it became abso-lutely a matter of necessity that either this fair-haired boy, or Rodgers, or myself should fight one of the insolent bullies.

And so this boy finally went at his work. He fought like a Trojan, and refused to cry out. He was beaten — mercilessly beaten. He had ex-pected that, but he refused to cry out, and the " tough's " friends, not so hard at heart, after all, interfered at last of their own will, and led both boy and bully, each one blinded from blood and bruises, down to the river bank, and, as they washed their wounds, praised my boy friend gloriously for his valor.

Ah, me, my fair-haired little " Lum," this was long, long ago; and your yellow hair, like mine own, is taking on the whiteness of the snowbanks that first knew our friendship. But, Lum Ray, I love you now as I loved you then. It was for me, a frailer boy, you fought, Lum Ray, years and years ago, on the bloody grass there by the bending river, and I lay this little tribute of thanks at your feet.

Reader, do you know that oftentimes I dislike to tell all that I might tell of these old days? I "tell the truth," but oftentimes not "the whole truth." The world has gone forward far in the path of civilization since then. Those terrific "fist-fights" were as common, and, indeed, almost as compulsory in those days, if you meant to maintain yourself, as the breathing of air.

And now let us speed forward with the conclusion of the war. After a ten-days siege, starvation, fights — both in camp among ourselves, and outside with savages that hovered unpleasantly close about — the long-expected re-enforcements came from the south. And then we feasted! And then we fought a little more among ourselves, testing the mettle of the new men, as it were; then another election; then bloody work began! for the new company had captured a small camp of Indians, and from them learned that there was a white woman prisoner on one of the islands in the great valley. And my heart was in my throat. Was it really she? What cared I for the desolated valley and the dead! What cared I if one or one dozen white women still survived the massacre? My only concern was, could it be this one, whose sad and silent face I had looked upon, this piteously beautiful girl?

CHAPTER XXIV.

THE LOST CAPTIVE.

Do you know that these Indians here used the *yew-wood bow of which the Bible speaks? Singular that the Modoc, the " yeoman " of Scotland and David's men in the Bible should alike have used the wood of the yew tree for their artillery!

But let us get forward to the battle in the water. The melting snow had made the Indians on the islands more than secure up to this time, for we had no boats; but now the waters had flowed on, and the low and fast subsiding condition of the spring freshet was making the place accessible on horses. On the last days of April we surrounded and " stormed " the island on horseback. In most places the water was too deep, and the men only lost their arms and their temper while floundering in the water. But two places were found where horses could keep their footing. A second charge was ordered, the mounted men taking only a single pistol this time in hand. This second charge was repulsed also, and not at all by the continued storm of arrows, but because our horses suddenly came

upon spears and elkhorns and sharp sticks that
pointed outward from the island. The water was
made bloody and ruddy from their wounds, and they
refused to go forward. At the third and final on-
slaught the men stripped to the waist, and waded to
their necks, advancing from every side and firing
their pistols only, while the men in the grass kept
firing at long range with larger artillery.

As for myself, I sat on a horse a little distance
back directing the fight. Suddenly I saw a great
commotion. Then boats shot out from every side.
It was a cunning and a most carefully planned
scheme, and brilliantly conducted on the part of the
Indians. " Save who can! " At first our men in
the water fell back. Then they rallied and fought
hand to hand, often up to their necks in the water.

Let it be confessed that it was a great satisfaction to see so many canoes filled with women and
children and old men dart through that band of
naked besiegers and escape to the wider waters,
the willows, the grass. But for all that the water
was red. It was the reading over again the bloody
page of Prescott, the Aztec, Cortez and his boats
on Tezcuco — the bloody water!

There was one little boat that I from the first
noticed with concern ; for it held a young woman,

who was singularly tall and slight and supple.
There was only one other person in this boat, a
bent old man.   Guided by the girl's strong, sure
hand, the craft got through the besieging party and
came to land a few hundred yards from where I
sat, the girl landing first, stooping low, running
forward leading the bent old man, almost dragging
him in her swift run through the long, green grass.
I plunged forward; my horse sank to his knees,
then to his belly.   I ran on after the fugitives on
foot.   I did not even draw my pistol from the holster.
My mission was of love; not of war!   But alas,
and alas, it was not she!   The bent old man was
badly shot, and made the water in which the rank
grass stood bloody as they ran.   He fell on his
back as I ran up, and kicked at me, trying to keep
me back for the girl to escape.   But she refused to
run.   She bent down over her father and held his
head up out of the water, glaring at me like a wild
beast.   Her black eyes literally blazed.   I turned
back and left them.

Out and up from the great rich valley of grasses
and flowers the Army of California rode on the first
day of May, leaving not one visible Indian behind.
Some of the horses were hung with scalps, as if
they had been hung in black fringe for a funeral.

The Army of Northern California, as it rode out and up from the valley through the glorious pines, was literally loaded down with scalps, with plunder and with vermin.

I left this wild string of howling human beings on the first day out, and struck through the wilderness alone for my own camp. I was fired upon from ambush almost immediately, but contrived to reach home; and, if the printer finds this MS. hard to decipher, let the bullet wound and the broken arm that I carried back with me be my excuse for its bad condition.

And that beautiful and silent lady there alone among the savages? Never another word or sign of her.

CHAPTER XXV.

UNTOLD TRAGEDIES.

I NOW saw that I had made a grave mistake. Indians are clannish. They may fight among each other like the other people of the earth; but let them be attacked by the common enemy, and they make common cause. I had fought against their brothers, and I was not to be at once forgiven for that. On the other hand, I had sympathized with the Indians. That also was a mortal crime, an unpardonable offense, in the eyes of the whites.

Those of the Northern States who will remember the feeling that once was held in the Southern States against those who sympathized with the blacks will understand something of the feeling in the West against those who take part with the Indians.

I had attempted to sit on two seats at once, and had slid between the two. It takes a big man to sit on two chairs at once. Any man who has the capacity to do such a thing, has also the good sense not to attempt it.

My wound was severe. It was nearly a year

before I was able to lift a hand.   Yet all this time
— what terror ! what tales of blood !

The Indians came slowly back into the country,
but some never came.   They had gone to the Pitt
River war.   The rank grass is growing above their
ashes on the hills that look upon that winding,
shining river.

Klamat was never friendly after that.   The
defeat of the Indians on all occasions, without
being able to inflict any injury in return, made
him desperate, and to see me among their enemies
did not add to his good nature.   But Paquita was
the same — the same gentleness in her manner,
the same deep sadness in her eyes as she tended
me.

The Doctor was a day's journey distant, safe out
of all the trouble and tragedy.   The Prince was
far away.   I was alone and friendless.   There was
not a day now that did not know some terrible
tragedy.   Three proud and warlike tribes of red
men were dying.   Their death throes were terrible.
Years and years after the events which I hastily
record, the armies of the United States antagonized
with a remnant of one of these tribes, the Modocs,
and made a red spot on the map that must remain
as long as history.   And it is by this alone that

you are to read the terrible things that I lived through in these early years. For I refuse to record the long and bloody struggle. Enough to say that there were battles fought here, battles that would make a book of tragedy and pathos, that are now entirely forgotten; for this was before the day of telegraphs and special correspondents, and all those who took part, save myself, the Indians on one side, and the miners on the other, have passed from the stage of action. Let us not linger, but hasten to the sad conclusion.

Little Klamat, now a man, and a man of authority, was in the front. That fierce boy, burning with a memory that possessed him utterly, and made him silent, sullen, and desperate, cared not where he fought or for whom he fought, only so that he fought the common enemy.

Paquita? What was she doing? Molding bullets! grinding bread! shaping arrow-heads and stringing bows! Maybe she was a sort of Puritan mother, fighting the British for home and hearthstone in the Revolution. Maybe she was a Florence Nightingale nursing the British soldiers in the Crimea.

I went down to the camp, where Klamat, Paquita, and about one hundred warriors, with a few women

who were nursing their wounded, were preparing
for the last final fight.   Here we waited till the
Modocs came down, and the three tribes joined
their thinned forces, and made common cause.

Women were gathering roots for their half-starved
children, children whose parents had been slain,
lost in the woods, and wandering they knew not
whither.

Shots were exchanged. The miners dismounted,
and fought on foot. The Indians shot wildly, for
they were poorly armed; the miners shot with
deadly precision.   Now and then a miner would be
carried to the rear, and now and then they would
charge up the hills or across the ravines, but that
was all that marked the events of the day till nightfall.

Toward nightfall the Indians, now entirely out of
ammunition, withdrew, leaving the miners, as usual,
masters of the ground.

Klamat had fallen in the fight, gun in hand, and
all his bravest warriors with him.

About midnight the women began to wail for the
dead from the hills. What a wail, and what a
night! There is no sound so sad, so heartbroken
and pitiful, as this long and sorrowful lamentation.
Sometimes it is almost savage, it is loud, and fierce,

and vehement, and your heart sinks, and you sympathize, and you think of your own dead, and you lament with them the common lot of man. Then your soul widens out, and you begin to go down with them to the shore of the dark water, to stand there, to be with them and of them, there in the great mysterious shadow of death, and to feel how much we are all alike, and how little difference there is in the destinies, the sorrows, and the sympathies of all the children of men.

We had not a single shot left, and but few arrows. While the old women were mourning their dead from the hills, the few remaining warriors, wounded, beaten, entirely broken in spirit, melted away in the dark, deep woods that reached up toward Mount Shasta.

I, too, could have escaped for a time in that direction. But that would only have continued the war and kept up the pursuit. For it was the white man, the terrible, bloodthirsty renegade, they wanted most of all. There could be neither truce nor peace while this man lived among the Indians.

There were a few strong horses left. Why not mount, and ride right down through the line at daylight to the banks of the river, swim the river, climb the precipitous crags on the other side, and escape to the south?

I spoke to Paquita about this as morning broke, and we could see the line of soldiers' camp that stretched between us and the river below. I assured her, that, once on the other side of that wide, deep water, I would be safe, for no man would risk his life to follow.

She said not a single word, but turned away with a sign that I should wait, and was gone.

Noon came and passed. Night was coming on. The soldiers were tightening a line around us. Had she, too, gone? Was I alone to be the sacrifice? Not another creature than myself was now to be seen in our camp.

Suddenly, through a cleft in a dense clump of cedars, she came, leading two horses. She had been waiting for the twilight to conceal her movements.

CHAPTER XXVI.

THE DEATH OF PAQUITA.

BUT what could she mean to do? why two horses?

She did not keep me long in suspense. Handing me the lariat of the stronger horse, she hastily and without a word threw herself on the other, and, beckoning me to follow, led hastily on straight down toward the river; for the soldiers were already in our rear, and closing around us fast. She struck straight down for the wide, deep river, as I had first indicated. She did not deviate or delay, but dashed, full gallop, right through the lines, and leaped boldly from the bank into the dark, swift waters.

It was a fearful leap; not far, but sudden and ugly, with everything against us. My horse and myself went far down in the blue, cold river, but he rose bravely, and struck out fairly for the other side.

But Paquita was not so fortunate. The river ran in an eddy, and her bewildered horse spun round and round in the whirlpool.

The soldiers discharged a volley as we disap-

peared, but I think neither of us were touched this
first fire.   My horse swam very slow, and dropped
far down the current.   The soldiers came up, stood
on the bank, deliberately loaded, aimed their pieces,
and fired every shot of the platoon at me, but only
touched my horse.   They had not yet discovered
Paquita, still struggling in the eddy, almost under
their feet.   At last she got her horse turned and
struck out, diving, and holding on to the mane.

She was not forty feet from the soldiers when discovered.   Pistols were drawn, and a hundred shots,
and still another hundred, rained down upon and
around the brave child.

I was down the stream out of reach, and nearing
the shore.   I witnessed the dreadful struggle, looking back, clinging to my wounded horse's mane.

She would dive, would reappear, a volley of shot,
down again till almost stifled ; up, again a volley,
and shouts and shots from the shore.

It seemed she would never get away from out
the rain of lead.   Slowly, oh how slowly ! her
wounded horse struggled on against the cold, blue
flood that boiled and swept about.

At last my spent horse touched a reach of sand
far below, that made a shoal from shore, and I
again looked back.

My horse refused to go further, but stood bleeding and trembling in the water up to his breast, and
I managed to make land alone. I crept up the
bank, clutching the long, wiry grass and water-
plants. I drew myself up, and sat down on the
rocks, still warm from the vanished sunshine.

When I had strength to rise, I went up the warm,
grassy river-bank, peering through the tules in an
almost hopeless search for my companion. Nothing was to be seen. The troops on the other bank
had gone away, not knowing, perhaps not caring,
what they had done.

The deep, blue river gave no sign of the tragedy
now. All was as still as the tomb. I stole close
and slowly along the bank. I felt a desolation that
was new and dreadful in its awful solemnity. The
bluff of the river hung in basaltic columns a thousand feet above my head ; only a narrow little strip
of grass and tules, and reeds and willows, nodding,
dipping, dripping, in the swift, strong river.

Not a bird flew over, not a cricket called from
out the long grass. " Ah, what an ending is this! "
I said, and sat down in despair. My eyes were
riveted on the river. Up and down on the other
side, everywhere I scanned with Indian eyes for
even a sign of life, for friend or foe. Nothing but

the bubble and gurgle of the waters, the nodding, dipping, dripping of the reeds, the willows and the tules.

If earth has any place more solemn, more solitary, more awful, than the banks of a strong, deep river, rushing, at nightfall, through a mountain forest, where even the birds have forgotten to sing, or the katydid to call from the grass, I know not where it is.

I stole further up the bank ; and there, almost at my feet, a little face was lifted, as if rising from the water into mine.

Blood was flowing from her mouth, and she could not speak.   Her naked arms were reached out and holding on to the grassy bank, but she could not draw her body from the water.   I put my arms about her, and, with sudden and singular strength, lifted her up and back to some warm, dry rocks, and there sat down with the dying girl in my arms.

Her robe had floated away in the flood, and she was nearly naked.   She was bleeding from many wounds.   Her whole body seemed to be covered with blood as I drew her from the water.   Blood spreads with water over a warm body in streams and seams ; and at such a time a body seems to be covered with a sheet of crimson.

Paquita!

I entreated her to speak. I called to her, but she could not answer. The desolation and solitude was now only the more dreadful. My voice came back in strange echoes from the basalt bluffs, and that was all the answer I ever had.

Blood on my hands, blood on my clothes, and blood on the grass and stones.

The lonely night was soft and sultry. The great white moon rose up and rolled along the heavens, and sifted through the boughs that lifted above and reached from the hanging cliff, and fell in lines and spangles across the face and form of my dead.

Paquita!

Once so alone in the awful presence of death, I became terrified. My heart and soul were strung to such a tension, it became intolerable. I bent my head, and tried to hide my face.

Paquita dead!

Our lives had first run together in currents of blood on the snow, in persecution and ruin, in the shadows and in the desolation of death; and so now they separated forever.

Paquita dead!

We had starved together; stood by the sounding

cataracts, threaded the forests, roamed by the river-
banks together ; grown from childhood, as it were,
together.   But now she had gone away, crossed
the dark and mystic river alone, and left me to
make the rest of the journey with strangers and
without a friend.

Paquita !

Why, we had watched the great sun land, like some
mighty navigator sailing the blue seas of heaven,
on the flashing summit of Shasta; had seen him come
with lifted sword and shield, and take possession of
the continent of darkness ; had watched him in the
twilight marshal his forces there for the last great
struggle with the shadows, creeping like evil spirits
through the woods, and, like the red man, make a
last grand battle there for his old dominions.   We
had seen him fall and die at last with all the snow-
peak crimsoned in his blood.

No more now.   Paquita, the child of nature, the
sunbeam of the forest, the star that had seen so
little of light, lay wrapped in darkness.

That night my life widened and widened away
till it touched and took in the shores of death.

Tenderly at last I laid her down, and gathered
fallen branches, decayed wood, and dry, dead
reeds, and built a ready pyre.

I struck flints together, made a fire, and, when the surf of light again broke in across the eastern wall, I lifted her up, laid her tenderly on the pile, composed her face, and laid her little hands across her breast.

I lighted the grass and tules. The fire took hold, and leaped and laughed, and crackled, and reached as if to touch the solemn boughs that bent and waved from the cliffs above, as bending and looking into a grave. I gathered white stones and laid a circle around the embers, and, while doing this, I discovered a canoe in the tules, which soon bore me away in safety.

How rank and tall the grass is growing above her ashes now! The stones have settled and settled till almost sunk in the earth, but this girl is not forgotten. This is the monument I raise above her ashes and her faithful life. I have written this that she shall be remembered, and this narrative should here have an end.

FINIS.